Tranny

911

Dixie's Rise

THE COMPLETE SERIES

By SHAY HUNTER

READ THE TRANNY 911 SERIES
IN THIS ORDER

EBOOKS:
TRANNY 911
TRANNY 911 2: THE FINALE'
TRANNY 911: DIXIE'S RISE
TRANNY 911: DIXIE'S RISE – PART 2

OR

PAPERBACKS:
TRANNY 911: THE COMPLETE SERIES
TRANNY 911: DIXIE'S RISE - THE
COMPLETE SERIES

Library of Congress Control Number: 2014930381
ISBN 10: 0989790177

ISBN 13: 9780989790178

Cover Design: Davida Baldwin www.oddballdsgn.com
Graphics: Davida Baldwin
www.thecartelpublications.com
First Edition

Printed in the United States of America

THIS NOVEL IS A PART OF

THE CARTEL PUBLICATIONS

A SUBSIDIARY OF
THE CARTEL PUBLICATIONS

CHECK OUT OTHER TITLES BY THE CARTEL PUBLICATIONS

What's Up Fam,

We hope that everyone had a great and safe New Year. 2014 is starting off beautifully. The Cartel Publications has a lot of new and exciting things in store for our fans so buckle up and enjoy the ride!

Jumping right into the novel on deck, "Tranny 911: Dixie's Rise". If you haven't read the first book, "Tranny 911", stop reading this and go cop it. You gotta see how Dixie got herself into the mess she's currently in. Charlie was having none of it and Dixie had to pay. Wait until you read what happens next.

Keeping in line with tradition, we want to give respect to a vet or trailblazer paving the way. With that said we would like to recognize:

Ne Ne Capri is the author of the hot series, "The Pussy Trap 1-3" and Co-author of, "Trust No Bitch". We love and respect Ne Ne's hustle and her support of The Cartel Publications movement goes beyond words. Make sure you check out her work.

Ok, go 'head and dive in! I'll get at you in the next novel.

Be Easy!
Charisse "C. Wash" Washington

Vice President

The Cartel Publications
www.thecartelpublications.com
www.twitter.com/cartelbooks
www.facebook.com/cartelpublications
Follow us on Instagram: Cartelpublications

Note to Readers

During your read of, "Tranny 911: Dixie's Rise", please keep in mind that the characters often refer to themselves as women because in their heart they are. Please don't get confused during the duration of the storyline by the use of exchanging feminine to masculine references.

Prologue

Dixie woke up staring at the ceiling and as usual he was in a horrible mood. It didn't make things any better that while his life was stagnant; Charlie was living as if he were royalty.

Hearing Charlie's cheerful voice day in and day out made Dixie's body itch. He wasn't the meek and sweet Charlie Dixie was accustomed to taking advantage of. He had grown. Every day was terrible with the new and improved Charlie but the current day was worse. Earlier that morning Charlie pranced around the house singing Luke's name on five different keys. Dixie was certain that Charlie was throwing his new boyfriend in his face and he longed for the day he'd get revenge.

Dixie created a plan the night before that he couldn't wait to put into action. He decided that he would place an anonymous call to the police and tell them that Charlie was responsible for the silicone injection deaths of Gi-Gi and Fergie, which occurred earlier that year. Dixie even decided to tell them where the bodies were buried.

When Dixie attempted to sit up in bed, he noticed he couldn't move. He tried again and again and the only motion he could deliver was the fluttering of his eyelids. When he tried to separate his lips he realized he couldn't even open his mouth to talk. What was going on?

When Charlie strutted into the room, Dixie tried to tell him that he was in trouble by moving his eyes but it didn't seem to be working. Couldn't Charlie understand that something was wrong and he needed help?

"Good morning, Dixon," Charlie said smiling down at him. He was holding a red pill bottle in his hand.

Dixie continued to roll his eyes rapidly, making every effort to communicate with Charlie but nothing seemed to work.

"I know what you're thinking right now," Charlie continued. "You're thinking, 'Why can't I move my body?' Well, let me help you understand—you can't move because I have given you something to paralyze you," Charlie shook the pill bottle, "courtesy of a dear friend of mine. And you will not move, unless I deem fit."

What the fuck does he mean? Dixie thought.

"And let me tell you why I have done this to you," he continued. "I found out a lot about you that I didn't know before—a lot of things I don't like. I discovered that you are evil, probably the child of the devil. And because of it, I don't trust you."

Charlie wiped the cascading curls out of Dixie's face. Just then Dixie noticed a huge diamond sitting on his finger. It was an engagement ring. The rock he was sporting explained why Charlie had been excited all day. Luke, Charlie's newfound love, proposed and Charlie must've said yes.

Dixie was devastated.

"I also know that you never had a heart murmur, Dixon. I know you been blackmailing me and trying to make me feel bad to control me and I know that will never happen again. I'm over you, Dixon. Those days are long gone, thanks to Sugar and my future husband," Charlie flashed his ring and a tear rolled down Dixie's face.

Tranny 911: *Dixie's Rise*

Dixie knew he was wrong for all of the games he played on Charlie's heart. At one point in time Charlie would've given his soul for Dixie's friendship but nothing seemed to be good enough. Dixie caused every relationship Charlie ever developed to shatter just so he would be the only one in his life. And now it was evident that all of his actions failed.

"To make sure that you will never hurt another person," Charlie said walking up to Dixie. "I am going to keep you paralyzed. I don't know if it'll be a few days, weeks or months. I do know that I won't stop the dosages until I can see that your eyes have changed." Charlie continued.

"Now I don't want you to worry about your care, even though I still have my clients that I have to take care of," he continued. "To ensure that you get cleaned and the like, I've hired a nurse who has no idea that I'm keeping you in this state. She'll help administer care when I'm out injecting my clients. Dixon, you have finally reaped what you sowed."

Charlie lifted Dixie's upper body and Dixie's arms lazily fell behind Charlie's back. With a loud grunt Charlie hoisted Dixie up and placed him into a wheel chair sitting beside the bed.

SHAY HUNTER

"This is going to be your new situation," Charlie said while pushing him toward the window. "Every morning I'm going to come in and take you out of bed. And I'll push you to this window, so that you can see life passing you by. And when I'm ready, only when I'm ready," he continued whispering in Dixie's ear, "your meds will stop." Charlie ran his hand over Dixie's face. "Don't be mad at me, Dixon. You always said you wanted me to take care of you, so here we are."

Charlie kissed Dixie on his silicone-injected cheek and walked out the door.

As Dixie stared out into the sunlight he knew one thing above all. He didn't care how long it would take, but at some point in his life he planned to pay Charlie back.

And he planned to do irreparable damage.

CHAPTER ONE

Dixie

Everyday I woke up unable to move my arms, legs and face, I got angrier. I didn't know what was worse, the condition I was in or the fact that I had to see Nurse Aggy's face six days a week.

Charlie hired Nurse Aggy, a tranny whose real name was Maggie, because she didn't feel like cleaning my piss and shit everyday. I guess keeping me paralyzed was more work than she thought and she didn't feel like breaking any of her precious fake nails.

Nurse Aggy wouldn't be so bad if she would stop talking to me. Instead of doing her work, which included cleaning my diapers and moving

SHAY HUNTER

my limbs, she took to telling me about her life in South Carolina which I couldn't care less about.

I knew all about how her mother disowned her when she found out that she had been sleeping with her husband, Aggy's stepfather, from the age of fifteen through twenty-five. Although she kicked her out of the house, her father didn't stop fucking her. Instead he shipped her to Washington D.C. to live and he paid her rent every month.

That wasn't the worst part about all of this mess. You should see this monster. I mean who was Nurse Aggy to have someone to care about her and love her when she wasn't even attractive? Why was I stuck to the bed like cum splat against the bathroom wall while this monster got to live her life? The anger I felt right now was so great it boiled over like grits in a hot pot. I needed a release and I needed a way out and now I had one. It came unexpectedly too.

It was raining hard outside the day things started looking up for me. Nurse Aggy had just finished moving my limbs so that they wouldn't stiffen after telling me a boring story. I found the physical therapy I was subjected to ridiculous since that fish Charlie had no intentions on letting me walk and was keeping me in this condition.

Tranny **911**: *Dixie's Rise*

Anyway, Nurse Aggy has a habit of curling her hideous wig before she got off work. On this particular day she was rushing to fuck her stepfather who had caught a flight into town and she was afraid she'd be late. When her cell phone rang she rushed to answer it and placed the iron on the chair next to me. It rolled off and fell against my leg.

The burning sensation I felt was unbelievable. There was no way I could tell her that I was in trouble because although I could move my tongue slightly, I couldn't move anything else...or so I thought.

As Nurse Aggy continued to talk on the phone and pace the room the iron continued to burn into my skin. I thought I would burn to death until I mustered enough strength to move my index finger. Up until that time I didn't think movement was possible. I had been trying for months to move my body and nothing seemed to work but my new movement came at a good time.

I flicked the iron with my finger so hard it fell on the floor. Nurse Aggy must've heard it because she turned around, rushed toward me and saw it lying on the floor. She looked horrified. When she looked down at my leg she saw the

SHAY HUNTER

burn and apologized over and over for her error. I didn't move my finger again because I didn't know if I could trust her with my secret. What if she told Charlie and he gave me more meds? She patched me up and since Charlie never bothered to look at my body he never found out.

Although Nurse Aggy claimed she was sorry she didn't bother to tell Charlie about the incident. She kept that little secret to herself and that's when I realized that this ugly, southern man monster had a sneaky side to her. If I could ever get out of this bed maybe I could play on it. Only time would tell.

I was lying in the bed as usual watching Nurse Aggy lift my legs back and forth. I could care less about my limbs because they weren't doing me any good. My focus was on my index finger. I worked it so much that it was stiffening and I was hoping I could move other parts of my body later. When she was done running her mouth she left and I spent the next two hours looking at the ceiling. Then there was a lot of noise outside of the bedroom. What was going on now?

When I heard laughter, I figured Charlie must've been having a party because I heard Belize, another tranny, and other voices in the living room. I couldn't believe Charlie was having people over the house when she knew she was keeping me paralyzed in the bedroom. I wondered what she told them about me because it wasn't like they didn't know we were roommates at one point. Did they think I left or did she say I was dead? It didn't matter because as of right now Charlie ruled my life. I was about to doze off until I heard Belize's voice getting louder. It sounded like she was in the hallway.

"Where did Charlie say the bathroom was again?" Belize yelled to someone.

"Straight in the back to the left," someone told her.

This was crazy. Charlie must've left people alone in the house, which was something she never did. Instead of going into the bathroom, I saw the gold doorknob twist clockwise and a few seconds later Belize was looking at me. Nurse Aggy must've left it unlocked by accident when she left.

"Oh, I'm sorry I didn't know anybody was..." she leaned in and walked closer to me. "Dixie, is that you?"

Belize's red wig, which was styled in a bun, sat high on top of her head. And the blue and white dress she wore was tight enough to show the masculinity of her chest and legs despite the socks stuffed into her bra, which were supposed to be tits.

I tried to move my eyes but I knew she would never understand me. My heart started beating rapidly because I figured this was the moment I was waiting on. Belize would see that something was wrong with me and go for help. If only I could let her know that I was being kept this way on purpose. I moved my finger but she couldn't see it and even if she did she probably wouldn't care.

"Are you okay?" she asked placing her hand over her heart.

I moved my eyes more.

"Can you talk, honey?" she sat on the edge of the bed and placed a hand on my leg. "Are you sick? Do you wanna watch some TV?" She grabbed the remote off of the dresser and placed it by my hand.

I continued to move my eyes wildly. My pupils throbbed from moving from left to right so much but it was the only way I could communicate. Belize looked confused and concerned and I hoped she would do something. Whether it be calling the police or getting me out of there, she had to make a move before Charlie got back. I needed something to go down now!

All hope was lost when I saw Charlie's slender frame slide into the doorway. Unlike Belize's, the black tight dress she wore accentuated her B-cup breasts, tiny waist and slender legs. Her face was just as perfect as a female model's, with her high cheekbones and large eyes. Beauty wasn't a problem for Charlie; the hate she had toward me was.

Charlie stepped into the room further and yelled, "Belize, what are you doing in here?"

CHAPTER TWO

Charlie

I was in a good mood when I came back from the liquor store with more Moscato until everyone said that Belize had gone to the bathroom about five minutes ago. I knew there was a possibility that she would go into the wrong room but I hoped that Maggie would've locked the door like she was instructed to do before leaving each day. But when I walked into Dixie's room and saw them together I knew I was wrong.

This entire thing with keeping Dixie paralyzed was starting to weigh on me. At first I wanted to keep her that way because of all of the evil things she'd done and the people she hurt, including me. But after awhile, when the hate wore off, I realized it was just to keep my secret safe and my ass out of jail.

And now here they were sitting together looking at me. I could tell when I walked into the room that Dixie was relieved. Belize was here to save her and it was all in her eyes.

"I was going to the bathroom and I came into the wrong room," Belize said standing up. She looked concerned with the bangs of her red wig draped over her left eye, giving her that sultry Lucille Ball look. "But what is going on here, with Dixie? I mean why is she like this?"

I walked further into Dixie's room. I glanced down at her and I could've sworn I saw a smile on her face. It was all in my mind, I'm sure, but it still horrified me that she was there. "It's not what it looks like, Belize."

"Well how about you explain it to me, sweetie? Because I'm confused."

"Dixie was in an accident that rendered her paralyzed," I said in a soft voice to conceal my lies. "She and I had our problems but I always took care of her. You know that. That was one of the reasons I almost said no when Luke asked to marry me. I felt bad leaving her alone in this condition, without any friends or family. So when this horrible accident happened I stepped up to be there. I didn't have any choice."

Belize, my dearest friend, looked deeply into my eyes. I could see she didn't believe me. "What kind of accident, Charlie?"

"What?"

"You said she was in an accident and I'm asking you what kind?"

I almost forgot about the lie I just told her. "It was a motorcycle accident. She got up with this motorcycle club and they were taking a trip to Virginia. She just learned to ride and went off the side of the road and crashed into a guardrail. It almost ended her."

"She doesn't look like she's been in an accident."

"She's been like this for months, Belize. So the main scars are healed but it was bad at first. Plus you know with her botched facial injections she didn't want anybody to see her like this but me."

She looked back at Dixie and then me again. "This doesn't seem right," Belize responded. "Something in her eyes makes me feel like something else is going on."

My brows lowered. "How you figure?"

Tranny 911: *Dixie's Rise*

"I don't know if you remember our last conversation about Dixie but I do. The last time I talked to you about her you told me she moved out of the state. Said you two couldn't get along so you made some firm decisions and that you wished her well but couldn't live with her. If that's the case then why is she in the bed looking like some washed up Broadway actress?"

I folded my arms over my breasts. "So you think I'm lying?"

"I never called you a liar, Charlie, and I'm not going to start now. But I will say things don't look right around here. You and I both know it."

"How long have you known me, Belize?"

"For about ten years, give or take two."

"Have you ever known me to beat around the bush or tell you a lie?" I asked. "Ever?" I screamed.

She shook her head no. "Not that I can think of."

"Well why would you start accusing me now? She was paralyzed and because of how she looked physically I put myself in a position to help her so that she could save face. Literally. If anything I deserve a medal for all I had to give up and do daily."

SHAY HUNTER

Belize looked at Dixie again and then back at me. She exhaled. "You're right, Charlie, and I'm so sorry. If you believe you are doing the right thing then so be it."

"I am doing the right thing."

"So when are you going to take her to a hospital for a check up? So we can make sure she's getting the proper treatment?"

"I have a nurse coming here everyday, Belize. Trust me when I say he's fine."

"But is she getting better, Charlie? Because it doesn't make a difference if she looks fine. Something could be going on internally that we can't see."

I love Belize and she knows I do. But the one thing I can't stand is somebody dipping into my personal business. There was no way I could let Dixie go to the hospital only for them to find out that I had been drugging him all along. I could end up in prison and away from Luke forever. And now here she was jumping in my face about Dixie's wretched ass. I was the one in charge of this situation not Belize or Dixie.

"Like I said everything is under control in here. There is a party tonight, Belize, and all I want to do is celebrate being Luke's wife with my girls. So let's go back out there and enjoy the party." I turned to walk away hoping she'd follow.

"Charlie," she yelled.

I turned back around. "Charlie nothing!" I fired back. "I'm not going to go against what Dixie wants by taking her to a hospital just because you're uncomfortable with this. Trust me when I say the nurse I have working with her will let me know if something is off. That's what I pay her for."

Belize looked into my eyes. "I have a feeling that things are going to get bad for you."

"Why? Because I won't do what you want me to do?"

I waited for the answer. She looked at Dixie again and then back at me. "It just doesn't feel right. And you are my friend and I'm going to always worry about you. Always. I've seen both the good and the bad that's happened to you over the years. As a matter of fact, I'm one of your biggest supporters in life and that will never change." She looked at Dixie again. "But I have a feeling if she remains where she is, like she is, she may die. I mean is that a chance you're willing to take?"

"I don't see it that way," I sighed.

"Then how do you see it?"

SHAY HUNTER

"I see the fact that I'm a saint in this shit. This dude was the worst person anybody could ever encounter and he should be happy that I care for him, see to it that he's nurtured and keep him alive. Everything is not as it seems, Belize."

"Can I ask you a question that I'll never ask again?"

I was nervous but decided to roll with it. "What is it?"

"Are you hurting him on purpose?"

She was on to me. How did she know? "Hurting him on purpose? Why would you even say some shit like that?"

"You haven't answered my question."

"No. I would never—"

When there was a clank on the side of Dixie's bed, we both turned around and looked at her. She was looking over at us. I slowly walked to the other side of the bed and saw a remote control lying down.

At first I thought he did that to alert Belize until I realized he couldn't move.

Belize walked up to Dixie's bed and leaned down. "What is it, Dixie? Are you trying to tell me something?"

Tranny 911: *Dixie's Rise*

CHAPTER THREE

Charlie

I was sitting in Flemings Steakhouse restaurant in Washington DC with my fiancé, Luke. I remember looking forward to this night a few days ago because we hadn't spent a lot of time together. I even picked out a beautiful red dress from Saks Fifth Avenue and a pair of sexy Christian Lou's for the evening in the hopes of seducing him later. But as I sat across from my perfect man, all I could think about was Dixie and Belize.

Yesterday when we were celebrating my engagement to Luke at my house and the remote control fell down on the floor in Dixie's room, it was trouble. I knew it fell on accident but Belize spent fifteen minutes trying to figure out if Dixie was trying to tell her something. Over and over she asked her questions as if she would finally answer. But I knew for a fact that she was paralyzed and that it couldn't be done.

Eventually I had to pull Belize out of the room and threaten to cut her out of my life for good if she didn't come with me. I hated doing that kind of shit but what else could I do? She wouldn't leave it alone.

Slowly she stood up off of the bed and looked down at Dixie. She looked back at me and said, "I know something is going on here. But because I love you, I'm going to let you figure things out the tough way. But be prepared to lose."

"So you know I have to go to church in a few days with my mother," Luke said as he cut into a hefty piece of steak. "But I'm not feeling it this time."

His voice was strong and authoritative like normal. His black New York baseball cap sat low on his face but I could still see the bottoms of his large brown eyes. When he picked up his glass of whiskey the muscle of his arm, which was covered in tattoos, buckled. I couldn't believe he belonged to me.

Tranny 911: *Dixie's Rise*

I wiped my hair behind my year. "Why not? You go to church with her all the time," I responded even though my mind was still with Dixie and Belize.

"I know but this time is different." He sat his glass down, removed his cap and sat it on the table. He sighed and I could tell he was frustrated. "She said it's important to her that the congregation sees her with family before they recommend her for the head of the Children's Ministry. And as much as I try to be there for my mother, I'm not feeling it right now."

"Maybe it's just me but I think you're making a bigger deal out of this than you're letting on," I said sipping my drink. "Unless you want to say something else that you aren't telling me."

"It's not that deep, baby. It's just that I feel like I'm being fake when I go into that church. You wouldn't believe how much they talk about homosexuality and shit like that. I feel like a fraud when I know that I am the one thing they hate more than anything. What happened to everyone being included based on their heart and not who they love?"

I wonder if Belize is going to tell everybody at Club Wiggles about Dixie being in the house.

SHAY HUNTER

Once that info gets out they won't let the shit rest and somebody will probably go to the police. I should've told her to keep it a secret but I wanted to get her out of there and away from Dixie. I fucked up.

"Baby," Luke yelled. "Are you listening to me?"

I jumped and looked into his eyes. He looked frustrated. He had probably been talking to me and I didn't hear what he was saying because I was in my head. "I'm sorry, Luke," I reached over and touched the top of his hand. "I was just think-ing about something that's all. What were you saying again?"

"What is it?" he asked in a concerned tone. "I mean what has your mind so strapped that you can't give me five seconds of your time when I haven't seen you in days? This isn't like you. So come out with it."

"It's nothing. Honestly."

"You're my woman, Charlie. And I don't like you having to deal with things on your own. I told you that when we first decided to be husband and wife. So if something is going on and I can help you with it I want to be there for you. Now what is it?"

I looked over his face. My eyes rolled down the tattoos on his neck and arms. I loved the art on his body. I loved his heart even more which was why I didn't want to tell him something that I was sure would break us apart. If I told him that I had Dixie held up in my house and was keeping her paralyzed would he think I was a monster? And more than anything would he still want to marry me?

"It's nothing you need to worry about, Luke. I have a few clients who have been giving me a hard time and they were on my mind. The home nurse care business I run is grueling and I'm sorry if I have been neglecting our relationship."

"How come I don't believe you?"

"Probably because you were talking to me and I zoned out. My business is tough and sometimes I take it home with me, Luke. I really am sorry."

"Baby, I keep telling you that you don't have to work. With the money I earn as a tattoo artist I can provide for us. You don't have to worry about anything but you have to stop trying to be the man and allow me."

Those words were funny to me. He wanted me to stop trying to be the *man*. How could I when I was one? He forgot all the time and it amazed me. All because I kept a long, flowing weave and sported tight jeans and high heels. Even if he could look through all of that, I still had the penis that I was hoping to get rid of by the end of next year. With all of the money I made in injections I would've done it a long time ago but he said he didn't want me risking undergoing surgery and dying. It wasn't like he touched my dick anyway. It stayed tucked between my legs when we made love so he could fuck me in the ass. But at the end of the day I was still a man whether he saw it or not.

"You know I can't quit my job, Luke. I love helping people because it—"

"Excuse me, do I know you?" a woman asked walking up to our table, interrupting our conversation.

I observed her dirty grey pantsuit, her wrinkled dark skin and her sad eyes. She was right; I did know her but from where?

"I may but I'm not sure," I admitted. "Who are you?"

"Do you know Christopher Ferguson?" she asked, her voice heavy with compassion.

"No...the name doesn't ring a bell."

Tranny 911: *Dixie's Rise*

She smiled as if she knew something I didn't. "I'm so sorry, honey," she chuckled softly. "First let me introduce myself, my name is Emma Ferguson and I remember seeing you at a party a few years ago that I threw for Christopher's birthday. Your name is Charlie, right?"

"Yes."

She grinned. "Good. I really want to extend my apologies again because sometimes I forget that my son has a full life and that people know him differently than I do."

I was waiting for the part that involved me.

"Like I was saying my son was born as Christopher but his friends call him Fergie."

My eyes widened and I could feel my right leg trembling. She had my attention now. It was as if the wind had been knocked from my body. Not only did I know whom Fergie was, I also knew where he was buried and that she would never see him again. Fergie's death was one of the main reasons I paralyzed Dixie.

Before he was killed, Fergie was Dixie's best friend. He was the only one who could put up with Dixie's shit and for whatever reason he trusted and loved him. That didn't matter to Dixie though because she killed Fergie while doing the injection procedure she saw me do twice. All for some money!

I will never forget the day I came home and saw Fergie gasping for air in my living room, probably due to the silicone traveling through his body and into his heart. Dixie didn't know how to do the procedure so she fucked up. I wanted to save Fergie's life and take him to the hospital but Dixie was afraid he would go to the cops. So we watched the life leave his body and later buried him in Strawberry field, a property that belonged to Dixie's family.

"You know Fergie...right?" she asked me.

"Uh...yes. I think so but I can't be sure."

She seemed disappointed. "But I remember you holding a conversation with him at the party. I even remember telling Fergie how beautiful you were." She paused. "Are you sure you don't know who my son is?"

I looked over at Luke and then back at her. "Uh...I...I mean...I think I remember him but he was more of a friend to Dixie than he was to me."

Her eyes widened with hope. "Oh, Dixon. How is he?"

I looked over at Luke who didn't know about any of this. I told him like I told everybody else…that Dixie moved out and left me the place alone. I don't know if he believed me but he didn't like Dixie enough to ask.

"I don't know," I said before taking a sip of my drink. "He moved out and I haven't seen him since."

She reached in her purse and handed me a white card with black lettering. "That's my contact information. If Dixie comes back anytime soon can you call me? It's urgent that I speak with him because I haven't been able to find my son."

"I'll take your number but I doubt I'll—,"

"What is your number?" she asked interrupting me again.

"Excuse me?"

"Your number…so we can stay in touch."

I unconsciously read off my number as she keyed it into her phone. "I don't mean to be brash but something happened to my son, Charlie. I can feel it in my body and I need closure. My boy and me were close and he was all that I had in this world. Without him I am nothing. So I will risk my life to get answers."

SHAY HUNTER

CHAPTER FOUR

Dixie

Ever since I saw Belize I started to believe that I would get out of this situation after all. Something told me that if I would just be a little more patient, Charlie would finally get what she deserved and if I was lucky maybe I'd be able to see it.

Nurse Aggy was sitting on the edge of the bed moving my left foot from left to right. As usual she was running her mouth and telling me more about her life than I needed to know.

"So you know I told you yesterday that Jack came in town to take care of me, right?" She paused for a second and then continued talking. "Well when he got here I told him my car wasn't working and he put a down payment on another one for me. It's a used white Honda but it's all mine." Nurse Aggy bragged.

"I'm telling you, that man loves me so much, Dixie," she continued. "But I always get the impression that something is missing. Like he's with me for another reason outside of love."

You're right, stupid bitch. He's with you because your asshole opens with no problem and you let him fuck you in every hole God gave you, including your ears.

"I want so badly to be the faggy he wants me to be. I mean he says I'm doing a good job but you can never tell with a man you know? You have to stay on your toes if you want to keep a nigga these days because there's always another bitch with a wetter mouth or warmer ass than you laying in wait."

She moved to my other leg.

"I had a dream about this entire scenario last night too...you know, with another nigga taking my man and all. In the dream we were together in the bed. He kissed me and told me he had finally decided he wanted to be with me instead of my mother. When all of a sudden some hot Judy with a fat ass came rushing into the room. He was beautiful, Dixie. So beautiful I wanted to rip up his face. This Judy went on and on about how Jack should leave me right before telling me I'll never measure up.

"I woke up in a cold sweat and Jack was in the bed with me, holding me and consoling me. That night we made love...*real love*. If you ask me last night was the best fucking session we had in years. I get the impression that he wants me to know he's there for me but I also feel like it won't last. I'm too happy."

This story was so fucking boring. I wished Nurse Aggy would just kill herself but she probably wouldn't because I wasn't that lucky. If only I was able to move something more than my finger—like my foot so that I could kick this fish off my bed—I would finally be able to get some sleep. Instead I gave in to the torture I had be subjected to for months.

When the house phone rang I silently thanked God. I would have a few seconds of relief from her non-stop ranting. No wonder she loved this job—she got to persecute gimps like myself and there was nothing we could do to stop her.

She hopped up from the bed in her usual jovial manner and dashed toward the phone on the dresser. I had no doubt it was Charlie checking to

Tranny 911: *Dixie's Rise*

make sure there were no updates or movements on my body. She probably wanted to make sure I was in the same hell she left me in this morning.

When I pushed the remote off of the bed with my finger the last time Belize was over the house, Charlie looked like she wanted to shit in that fly ass dress she was wearing. I didn't think about it until later that pushing the remote was probably a bad idea, and that because of it Charlie may be suspicious that I could move.

The next day she tried to give me double the pills she normally did to keep me stiff. But there was something else on my body I could move more than I could before: my tongue. Although I couldn't talk, I could push out pills.

I had to take my time, and I do mean a lot of time, but I slowly pushed the pills out of my mouth. I learned that in order to make sure that they fell behind my head I needed to use a lot of spit before they exited my mouth so that they could slide down my cheek and behind my neck, otherwise they would get stuck on my face. I had to be diligent too. If I left the pills in my mouth too long they would dissolve and take effect and I would probably lose access to my finger again. I didn't have anything else to do with my time so it

SHAY HUNTER

was cool with me. In total I had pushed a total of twenty pills behind my head. If I kept it up I was hopeful that I would be able to walk again soon.

Nurse Aggy never noticed the pills when she cleaned my linens each week because she was so busy running her mouth. She simply pushed me in a chair, bunched the sheets up and threw them in a pile to wash on a weekly basis. I figured if I continued to get away with this, I would be up and ready to get revenge on Charlie and everything she loved before the year was over.

"Hello," Nurse Aggy said placing the phone on speaker. "Who goes there?"

"Hello, I'm looking for Dixon."

The moment I heard the voice of the woman on the other end my heart rate went up because I knew it all too well. The voice belonged to Emma, Fergie's mother, and I wondered how she got the number.

Nurse Aggy looked at me. I guess because I didn't normally get calls since nobody gave a fuck about me being alive or dead. In other words my social life was non-fucking-existent.

"Dixon is unable to come to the phone right now," Nurse Aggy said in an unconfident tone. "How did you get this number?"

Tranny 911: *Dixie's Rise*

"Charlie gave it to me."

"Are you a friend?" Nurse Aggy inquired.

"Are you saying that Dixon is there?"

"Yes," she responded rolling her eyes. "He's here. Just unable to speak."

"Are you sure he's there? Because someone told me that he moved away."

Nurse Aggy giggled. "Honey, I have a lot of things going wrong with me but bad eyesight ain't one of them. Dixon is here. Now may I take a message? I'll be able to give it to him later."

"Can I come see him?"

She looked at me and then shrugged. "I don't see why not. I'm sure he'd love the company. I know I would. As a matter of fact let me give you the address right now."

As I listened to Nurse Aggy recite the address, I thought about one thing, the fact that when Charlie got wind of this shit she was going to hit the fan.

I had a reason for feeling that way. I'd heard Charlie tell Nurse Aggy over and over that nobody was to know that I was paralyzed so I didn't understand why she was giving out the address. Nurse Aggy was green so maybe she thought that because Emma had the number, it was okay. After

all, nobody else ever called me. And since Charlie
gave it to her maybe she agreed I could use some
company. Why else would Charlie give her the
number? That's something even I wanted to
know.

Nurse Aggy ended the call after giving Emma all of the information she needed to find me.
She flopped back on the bed and started massaging my arm, the one with my moving finger. I decided to open up to her.

Now I knew I had this skill before but I never shared it with Nurse Aggy because I wasn't
sure if I could trust her. But since she never told
Charlie how she burnt me with the curling iron,
and it was obvious that she liked me, I decided to
go for it and take a chance. So the moment my
hand was inside of hers, I moved my finger.

Nurse Aggy screamed, dropped my hand and
held both sides of her face. "Dixie, how did you
do that?" she yelled.

I moved my eyes from left and right rapidly.
I didn't know what else to do and it was hard to
express myself, which was a problem I never had
in my life before this shit. I always said what was
on my mind, but now I had to get creative. Now
things were different.

Tranny 911: *Dixie's Rise*

I stopped moving my eyes and just stared at her.

"Are you trying to tell me something, Dixie?" she asked slowly. "Please say something because you're scaring me. You aren't supposed to be able to move."

I moved my eyes from left and right again.

Her eyes widened and her jaw dropped. "Okay...okay...let me think." She looked around the room. "What can I use to help you communicate with me?" She stood up and walked around the room.

I was beyond interested because I had been trying to find a way to talk to this ugly man bitch for the longest. So if she could come up with something, she would be rewarded. In fact if she could think of something I would never call her dumb or ugly again and perhaps I would keep her around for my benefit once I could move. But first she had to find a way to connect with me.

"I got it," she yelled the moment I had the thought.

She rushed out of the bedroom and returned with a white hand mirror that Charlie and I used to check the back of our Gilda's before we left the house. When she placed the mirror down on the bed she rushed back out. Then she came back with a small bowl of what looked like ketchup. She sat on the edge of the bed and looked over at me.

"Okay, can you spell? If you can move your eyes."

What type of dumb ass question was that? Of course I could spell! Just because I couldn't move didn't mean I was like this all of my life.

Instead of getting angrier I moved my eyes again and even rolled them.

"Good," she clapped her hands together. "I'm going to place your finger in the ketchup and I want you to spell what you want me to know on this mirror okay?"

I moved my eyes.

"Cool."

She took my finger and placed it into the cold condiment. I could feel my heart rate increasing because this was the closest I had ever gotten to getting out of this situation. Please let this work.

Four times she placed my hand into the ketchup and then the mirror. And when I was done she looked up at me with scared eyes.

"Oh, my God, Dixie." She paused. "You spelled HELP!"

Tranny 911: *Dixie's Rise*

CHAPTER FIVE

Charlie

I was driving ninety miles per hour in my candy apple red Mercedes Benz on the highway. I had just finished up a facial procedure when Maggie called and said I had to come home because it was urgent. I was already on edge because I asked my client, a tranny from North Carolina, if she smoked and she lied and said no. But I had done enough silicone injections now to know the difference. The moment I injected her face to give her fuller cheeks, the silicone slid down to her chin. It took me an hour to make her decent. Lying bitch!

Bad skin, which occurs from daily smoking, doesn't hold the silicone and sometimes it moves a little. Bitches love lying but complain later when the silicone doesn't sit right. Luckily for her, Kenny was the best artist ever and taught me everything I needed to know. In the end her face was firmer than it was the day she was born and she couldn't help but to keep thanking me. With that problem out of the way, it sounded like I was about to face another one.

I was about five miles from the house when my car phone rang again. I hit the button so that the speaker would come on and I could remain hands free. "Hello."

"Bitch, I been calling you all day! Where the fuck you been that you can't answer my call?"

I sighed because I didn't need this shit right now. "Hey, Belize. I couldn't come to the phone and I'm kinda busy at the moment."

"Hey, Belize shit. How you expect me to make sure you have the best wedding ever if you don't return my calls? That's so rude and I know somebody raised you better than that. If they didn't, I got a few minutes—come on over here and I'll beat some sense into you right quick."

I rolled my eyes and cut over in front of a mini van that was going five miles per hour. "If I could've answered the phone I would have, trust me. But this chick who I had an appointment with lied about her medical history and I almost fucked her face up. I needed to give her my full attention and now you have it so what's up?"

She sighed. "When are you going to realize what you do is not a real job?"

"Are you serious?" I frowned. "Are you actually calling me to browbeat me about what I do for a living?"

"I'm dead serious, Charlie. I thought the plan was to tuck enough money to buy a nice house, get your sexual reassignment surgery and get out. That lifestyle you leading doesn't have a long term plan and there ain't but one-way out and that's jail. You know that."

"Okay, mother," I said rolling my eyes.

"Okay, mother shit. If you gonna call me anything call me Mommy Dearest. At least have the comparisons on point."

I laughed. "Belize, Mommy Dearest, or whatever else you want to be called, you know you can't run my life. No one can. My own fiancé can't even tell me what to do. Do you realize he's still asking me to move in with him and to quit my job? And each time I tell him the same thing...no."

"Why haven't you?"

SHAY HUNTER

"Because this is my life…not his."

"Then you a fool. Because a nigga that fine would never have to ask me twice." She paused. "Anyway, I was calling to say that everything is set for your rehearsal dinner. All you have to do is call Ms. Monte with a credit card. Can you work that out or do you want me to pick up the money and pay it myself?"

"You mind? Because it will help me out a lot."

"For you, my dear princess, anything."

After I got off of the phone with her I parked my car in front of my house, opened the door and rushed into the living room. I tossed my purse on the recliner and walked over to Maggie who was sitting on the couch. A pot of coffee was in front of her on the table and her right leg was shaking rapidly.

"What's going on, Maggie?" I asked staring down at her. "Is everything okay with Dixie?"

"I want to tell you something else first before we get into Dixie. Someone named Emma called here for him. She said you gave her the number."

My body dropped down in the recliner and since my purse was there I sat on top of it. It was uncomfortable but I couldn't move. I don't know what I was thinking about when I gave Emma the number to the house. I was so nervous when she asked that I rattled off the only number I could remember, the house phone. In my haste I forgot to remind Maggie not to give anybody any information about Dixie but I hadn't expected Emma to call so quickly. I just saw her the other day.

"What did you tell her?" I asked looking over at him.

"Just that Dixie was unavailable."

"By unavailable do you mean Dixie was here?"

"Yes."

"Why did you say that?" I yelled. "I told you not to tell anybody that he was here. What is wrong with you?" I screamed so loudly my head throbbed. "I paid you to do a basic job and you can't seem to do it!"

"She had the number, Charlie. How was I to know it was somebody you didn't want to know about Dixie? Nobody ever calls here."

"When I say don't tell anybody anything I mean *anybody*," I screamed. I placed my face in my hands. "You have no idea what you just did. None at all."

SHAY HUNTER

"I know you're upset but there's a bright side to all of this," Maggie said with a smile on her face. "Dixie moved today."

I stood up and walked over to her. "What do you mean he moved?"

"Just what I said. He moved."

"Fuck," I yelled boxing at the air.

"Charlie, what's going on here?" Maggie asked in a concerned tone. She stood up and approached me. "Why don't you want people to know where Dixie is and why aren't you happy that he's showing progress? Shouldn't it be a good thing?"

"Yes…but…uh…"

"Then what's up with your attitude?" she paused and grilled me like either a mother or a lover. I couldn't be sure. "Are you hurting him?"

I placed my hands on my hips and walked so close to Maggie my new breasts pressed firmly against her sock filled chest. "Why would you ask me some shit like that? If I was hurting him on purpose why would I have you here?"

"To clean up after him, administer his feeding tube and stuff like that," she said with an attitude. "You too busy to do those things remember?"

Tranny 911: *Dixie's Rise*

This bitch was trying me and I had to put her in her place quickly. "Who do you think you are? Huh? It's my money you get every fucking week, not Dixie's! And if the fuck I tell you to do a job you better do it right. And that includes keeping my business private! Am I clear?"

"You are hurting him, aren't you?" she said slowly. "I can feel it."

I took one step back. Not because I was afraid but to look over her disposition. The way she stood in front of me. The way her shoulders squared off something was different. She'd built a connection with him I could tell. My only thing was how? It wasn't like Dixie could talk so what was so precious about him that Maggie would risk everything, including her job? Whatever it was I decided that it wasn't important enough for me to give a fuck about. This bitch had to go!

"I want you out of here."

"Okay. The only reason I stayed around anyway was to tell you about Dixie. I'll be back tomorrow."

"No, cunt, you don't understand…I want you out of here for good. You're fired."

Her shoulders slumped and her voice trembled. "But why? You don't have to do this. I've

SHAY HUNTER

made progress with Dixon and he's doing better with me around."

"I want you gone because I can't have an employee who defies me. You can stop by Friday to pick up your paycheck but you are no longer wanted. Now get out."

She paused and looked me over. "Okay. If you want me gone I'm out." She nodded her head up and down softly. "But you should know that I'm going to the police when I leave here today." She grabbed her jacket and her purse.

"Going to the police for what?"

"Because I want to make sure Dixie is okay. It would be different if I was still gainfully employed but since I'm not I'll—"

This slut was sneakier than I thought. "Okay," I yelled.

"Okay what?" she asked slyly.

"Okay you can keep your job."

She grinned. "Thank you. I really do think it's best for Dixie if I remain around."

I knew she felt like she won and at the current moment it appeared that way, but she didn't know me. She didn't know me at all.

"I apologize how I came at you too, Maggie," I said in a fake tone. "I had a rough day. And

I know things look crazy around here and you'll never begin to understand what I'm dealing with even if I told you. Just know that the person you are taking care of is dangerous. Very dangerous. And if I were you I wouldn't be too quick to care about him. I'm warning you."

SHAY HUNTER

CHAPTER SIX

Dixie

SIX MONTHS LATER

Nurse Aggy was massaging my hands and ironically enough I started looking forward to her company. It's as if we both knew a secret no one else did—I could communicate. If only I could get her to stop talking about dumb shit she would be halfway okay to be around.

"You know he broke up with me yesterday, right?" she asked me with a tear running down her cheek. "I'm a single girl and it hurts so badly. I guess my dream was right after all…about him leaving me and all."

I moved my fingers on my left hand to tell her that I was listening.

Tranny 911: Dixie's Rise

"Aw, thank you, my Dixie," she said wiping the tear away.

Although Charlie took over the pill duty every morning I still pushed them out of my mouth. And even though I wasn't sure if Nurse Aggy knew it was the pills that kept me paralyzed, she helped me throw them away. Especially after she told me how Charlie tried to fire her and she dug into her shit. I was surprised Nurse Aggy was still around but I knew it wouldn't be for long. We had to get me moving if I was going to have a chance to escape.

I even asked Nurse Aggy to push me in the wheelchair and take me out of here but she said she was too scared. However, she would help me walk out. So that was the plan. If I wanted out I had to stop taking the pills and move.

"Dixie, I don't know what I did to make him leave me. The last time I talked to him he said he was thinking about leaving my mother and moving out here with me. Said she was getting old and that he couldn't stand looking at her body anymore. The next minute he's telling me that he doesn't know if he's gay or not."

I know all too well those who claim they aren't gay every time life gets down on them.

SHAY HUNTER

Usually it occurs if the woman in his life makes him go to church, or somebody said they caught him out somewhere with a man. No matter what, I always knew that relationships with men are short lived. It's not about love like it is with the dyke's. It's all about the sex and who could give it to you better.

"If he leaves me I'm going to die, do you hear me? Just die. Who's going to love me like he does? I'm not an attractive woman. I'm not even smart. All I ever knew was how to love hard and make love."

When her hand was next to mine on the bed I eased three fingers toward her and gripped one of her fingers softly. She looked up at me because I had never done that before. Thanks to her, I was getting life in both of my hands and I wanted her to see her handy work.

A tear rolled down her face just as Charlie walked into the door.

"Maggie, I forgot to give Dixie her medicine. Can you see to it that she has it? I'm late for a fitting for my wedding dress and I can't do it right now."

Nurse Aggy took the pill from her and said, "Of course. You go take care of what you need to. You know I have Dixie."

Charlie walked toward the door to leave but stopped short and looked at me before looking at Nurse Aggy. "Maggie, it is very important that she takes the pill. One of the reasons she had the finger movement six months back was because of this medicine. If she doesn't have it she might not get better."

"Trust me, I got it," Nurse Aggy said slyly.

Charlie smiled at her and then left.

When the door was closed Nurse Aggy looked at me. I squeezed her hand tighter so that she knew I was afraid for my life. "Don't worry, I'm not going to give you anything that witch hands me, you know I don't trust her." She threw it in the trashcan.

I felt an immediate sense of relief. I had been pushing those pills out of my mouth on a daily basis and I didn't want to lose everything I was able to do with my body because she kept pushing those pills on me.

"You want to talk, Dixie?"

I gripped her hand.

SHAY HUNTER

"Okay, let's have a longer conversation this time. I want you to tell me everything you can about your life here."

When she went and got the ketchup and the mirror I took my time to spell everything that happened to me, in my version of course. I explained how I was more beautiful than Charlie, which made her jealous. I explained how she messed my face up so that I would be less attractive.

I could tell by looking into Nurse Aggy's eyes that she didn't believe that I was more beautiful but she didn't say anything. Everyone always thought Charlie was so beautiful and looked so much like a girl, except me. If you ask me her cheeks were too high, her titties were too round and her face is too porcelain-like.

The thing Charlie didn't realize was that in our life there was being *like* a girl and being a girl. She would never be a woman no matter how many times she got proposed to or married.

In the end, after about an hour I let Nurse Aggy know that Charlie was keeping me that way to prevent me from snitching on her. To prevent me from telling people how she botched my injections and even murdered a few people. I told her that I knew where their bodies were and that she should be very afraid of Charlie's alluring beauty.

"But why didn't she kill you?" Nurse Aggy questioned. "If she's such a murderer and all?"

I wished I could curse her out for questioning me. Instead I looked down at my hand and she placed it in the ketchup and then on the mirror until my message was done.

I spelled, "Because there's only one thing he likes more than murder. Torture."

She looked over at me and said, "What kind of evil beauty is this Charlie person? I don't understand."

I moved my finger again so that I could spell another message. "One you never want to cross."

SHAY HUNTER

CHAPTER SEVEN

Charlie

Monday talks way too much, which is why when she asked for a touch up on the silicone injections I gave her six months ago it was hard for her to catch me and get an appointment. I'm a perfectionist and when I'm pushing a needle into someone's body I need extreme concentration. Apparently Monday trusted me enough to break my tunnel vision with her mindless chatter.

She lay across the bed with her ass in the air as I tried to do my thing. I had done ten injections to make her ass fatter and had thirty more to go.

"Charlie, you wouldn't believe how many niggas, that deal with dudes, want to fuck me. I'm starting to wonder hard now."

"Why wouldn't I believe you?" I asked as I pressed some crazy glue on one of the injections sites I just made in the flesh of her ass cheek. "They try to come on to me everyday and most of them know I'm a guy."

"I believe you and it's crazy. My thing is this…I don't have a problem with you being with another dude if that's your thing. But if you gonna fuck niggas, don't try to slide up in me raw."

"Maybe you shouldn't fuck niggas who deal with faggies period. That way you can be safe."

"But I don't be finding out that they gay until after they get the pussy. I swear to God niggas is treacherous. You hear me?"

I rolled my eyes and stuck the flesh of her ass with my next injection. "I hear you."

"I'm going to tell you the real tragedy about all of this foolishness. When there be dudes like you who look better than us bitches. I mean damn, y'all be snagging all the niggas." She chuckled. "Leave some for a sister who want a family."

I stopped what I was doing and looked down at her. "First off, I ain't no nigga. I'm a woman no matter what was or is dangling between my legs." I stabbed the needle into her ass a little harder than necessary.

SHAY HUNTER

"Ouch," she yelled.

"Sorry," I lied.

"It's cool. And I ain't mean no disrespect by it, Charlie. I'm sorry if you think I did. I'm just saying what's on my mind. Y'all can be fooling the hell out of dudes if y'all want to. I mean look at your face and shit. I can't tell the difference."

"Thank you, I guess."

This bitch was hating big time and I will be glad when I finish. If I wasn't a perfectionist I would've injected a nice lump in one of her cheeks, which would fuck up the way her jeans look forever. But that ain't my steez.

Although she was off the chain, she was right. The battle between biological women and tranny's has been going on for centuries. We want what they have: the ability to be real women, to bear children, to have families without the pink elephant in the room that we're men. And they want what we have: sex appeal, style, and more than anything confidence to do us regardless.

"And then you had the nerve to pull Luke's fine ass," she continued. "I mean do you know how many bitches was trying to get at that nigga before word got out that he was gay?"

"I don't care about other bitches but if you must, do tell," I said sarcastically.

"So many females I know be looking at Luke and swearing they could turn him around. But guess what, at the end of the day you were the one who came out on top of that. You had him and the rest had to deal with it. I know so many broads who wanted to get at your face, slice it up and everything because you snagged him."

I stopped what I was doing. "What you mean slice up my face?"

"Don't worry, girl. It was some shit that a few chicks at the hair salon said when they first found out y'all was going to get married some time back. It ain't like it makes a difference now because y'all not together anyway, right?"

"Not together?" I smirked before inserting my next to last injection. "How you figure?"

Monday grew silent which was something she never did. I placed the last injection in her ass, added the crazy glue on her cheek to prevent leakage and pressed a cotton ball to her skin.

"Monday, what are you talking about we aren't together?"

"I'm sorry, Charlie. I really thought y'all broke up." She got up off of her stomach and walked over to her loose fitting black sweatpants. "Especially since he be at my church with that other chick."

"What other chick?"

"I'm not trying to get involved in y'all's—"

"What other chick?" I yelled in my deep man voice, which I never used. This startled her. "Stop playing games and tell me what you obviously want me to know anyway."

"That's just it, I don't know anything. The only thing I know for sure is that he goes to church every Sunday with this real girl." She covered her mouth. "Not saying that you aren't real but I mean a woman born as a woman. Damn, Charlie, I thought y'all was through."

I made it to New God Order Baptist church in Laurel, Maryland just as the doors were opening and church was letting out. I knew Monday was probably lying but I needed to confirm for myself. That's one thing about bitches, especially those who are mad you look better than them; they are always looking for an opportunity to shoot you down just because they're insecure.

As people filed out of the church I tried to look around for the man who belonged to me. It didn't take me long to see his mother come out first. She was so stunning. The auburn weave she got sewn in last week matched her complexion and her smile was bright and wide. And then I saw him...Luke. On his arm was a ravishing female. Her long, black hair hung down her back and brushed against the red dress she wore. She took my breath away and since Luke held onto her hand, she took my heart away too.

"I can't believe you're doing this shit to me," I said to myself trying to prevent from hyperventilating before approaching him.

My pride told me to get back into my car and drive home to cry my eyes out in private. But he belonged to me and I wanted him to know that I knew about his betrayal so that he wouldn't be able to deny it in the future.

So I parked my car, eased out and walked straight up to Luke. He was all smiles until he saw me. "I thought you would never hurt me! You promised!"

He pushed the girl aside and stepped toward me. "Baby, I—"

SHAY HUNTER

I slapped him in the face so hard it silenced any future statement. When I was done I stomped back to my car and pulled away. I always knew he was too good for me. Why would I think that I'd be able to keep him? Luke deserved to be with a woman like...like the one on his arm. One who could have kids and give him the life he wanted, the life he deserved.

As tears continued to roll down my eyes I tried to understand why he would propose to me. He could've been with her all along and saved me the pain. I guess it didn't matter anymore because I was done with him. Forever.

CHAPTER EIGHT

Charlie

I was lying face down on my bed with a pillow over my head. I had been crying ever since I caught Luke cheating earlier today and I felt as if my life was coming to an end. How could he do this to me? How could he do this to us? We were supposed to have the life and he stole it from me. I should've killed him. I should've taken his last breath and killed myself too. *What am I talking about?* I was so lost.

I rolled over and looked up at the ceiling. Everything reminded me of my relationship with Luke and I couldn't think about life without him but I guess I didn't have a choice.

I grabbed the phone on the dresser beside the bed and called Belize. I knew she was working

SHAY HUNTER

overtime to make my wedding a success so I needed her to know that the entire thing was off. The phone rang five times and she didn't answer. I was about to leave her a message until Maggie walked into the doorway of my bedroom.

Ever since she blackmailed me I didn't trust her but what could I do? If I fired her, she would go to the police and I didn't need them around, especially with Dixie being paralyzed.

The messed up part was that before our little run in I liked Maggie. I thought she was a stand up professional and a nice person. Now I didn't trust her past her ugly face.

I wasn't worried about too much though, because as long as I continued to stuff the pills down Dixie's throat her situation would remain the same. Always.

"Are you okay?" Maggie asked me. "I heard you come in about an hour ago. I was going to leave you alone but you're still crying. Did something happen?"

"It's nothing," I said trying to hold myself together. "I was just feeling sick that's all."

She stepped deeper into my room without an invitation. "Charlie, I know we've had our differences but I've always respected you and I look up to you. I'm here if you need me and I give great advice."

"I don't want to impose."

"Nonsense. Dixie is asleep and you don't have to be alone. I'm a great listener so talk to me. Tell me what's wrong."

I sighed. She wasn't the first person I wanted to tell my problems to but I really wanted to talk to somebody. "Why do men cheat?" Tears rolled down my face. "If you give them everything they want, why do they still leave you stranded? I don't understand. I'm a good woman and I deserve so much more."

She exhaled. "That's a good question but it truly depends on the man and the situation."

"I'm talking about my man. I found out today that he had another woman. The messed up part is that the entire time he was telling me that he wanted to marry me and that he'd never leave my side. I'm fucked up right now, Maggie. I feel like my world is coming to an end."

"Did you talk to him?"

I recalled how I slapped him and kept it moving. "I didn't have time."

"I really think you should speak to him first, Charlie. Sometimes there are reasons we can't see for things. I've seen you with Luke and I've never gotten the impression that he didn't love you. Whenever I see y'all together it gives me hope that it's possible for somebody like me to have a relationship as strong as yours. Don't let it go without a fight."

"Don't get too excited because our entire re- lationship was obviously bullshit," I said sitting up in the bed. "He fooled me and made me think that he loved me when all he was doing was play- ing with my mind."

Maggie looked at me and asked, "Can I sit down?"

"Yes."

She sat on the edge of the bed. "Charlie, there are a lot of things that go into a relationship. And I'm not telling you this to school you, or to make you think that you aren't smart enough to figure this out yourself. But you have to give a little in relationships. People make mistakes. Peo- ple fuck up and most of the time it has nothing to do with the heart. Talk to Luke. Talk to your man."

"By give a little do you mean compromise myself and let him have another bitch?"

Tranny 911: Dixie's Rise

"Of course not. Luke seems to be a great guy but you are a great person too. The only problem with the situation is the fact that you want to end the relationship instead of fighting for him. Compromise by giving him the conversation. And if after that it doesn't work, you'll know you tried."

"It's so hard."

"I know but I haven't seen a relationship that hasn't had troubles. Add to that the fact that you both are men and you're just begging for issues." She giggled. "But Luke seems to be different. He's over here almost every day and when he's not you're over there. I'd hate to see you lose a good man to a fish who doesn't know what to do with him."

Although I knew I wouldn't call Luke right now I appreciated that Maggie wasn't a hater. A lot of the time tranny's didn't want you happy because they were miserable. I was starting to think I was wrong about her and was glad that she stuck around. I didn't know what I planned on doing with Luke but I did know I was going to give it some more time.

"Thank you, Maggie. I got a lot to think about but—"

SHAY HUNTER

There was a knock at the door and I figured it was Belize. Since she started planning the wedding she stayed coming over my house to see if I could fit certain garbs. It was annoying and telling her the wedding was off would be the best part about the entire situation.

"Can you get the door, Maggie? I kinda want to be left alone right now."

"No problem. I'll make them go away. You just get some rest."

When Maggie left I crawled back under the sheets, preparing to cry my eyes out. I knew I had a long road ahead of me because before Luke I never imagined finding real love. Now that I had it, I didn't want it to be over.

When I rolled over to my left side I heard Maggie yell, "You can't come in here!"

Not knowing what was going on, I hopped out of bed and rushed toward the living room. The person standing before me caused my belly to cramp. I knew her. I knew her all to well. It was Emma Ferguson but what I didn't know was how she got my address.

Her hair was all over her head and her eyes were red like she'd been drinking and crying for weeks.

Tranny 911: Dixie's Rise

"Emma, what are you doing here?" I asked standing in front of her.

Maggie stepped out of Emma's way and walked toward Dixie's bedroom.

"Where is he?" Emma asked.

"Where is who?"

"Dixon. I know he's here so stop playing games!"

"Dixon is not here now you have to get out of my house!"

I walked toward the front door and opened it hoping she'd follow. Instead she ran toward the back of the house and toward Dixie's room. Maggie came outside and blocked her path before she got into Dixie's room, which forced her to remain where she was.

"Where is Dixon," Emma asked Maggie as tears rolled down her face and hung on her chin.

"He's inside the room sleep."

My jaw dropped. What was Maggie trying to do? I knew it was evident that I didn't want her here so what was she doing? Just when I had given her some props. I had plans to deal with Maggie later. I didn't care who she would tell. At this point if she went to the cops it wouldn't matter

SHAY HUNTER

anyway because I was sure Emma would say something.

"You need to be clear on something, I am not leaving here without seeing Dixie." She looked back at me and then at Maggie. "And I suggest you two don't try and stop me."

Maggie exhaled. "Okay, you can go look at him if you want to." She opened the door and Dixie was in the bed looking at us.

"Dixon," Emma said walking into the room cautiously. "Where is Fergie? Please talk to me. I've been looking all over for him." Dixie moved his eyes but did not speak. "Dixon, where is my son?" When Dixie didn't respond Emma looked back at Maggie, confused. "What's wrong with him?"

"He's paralyzed," Maggie said softly. "That is why Charlie didn't want you to know. Dixie couldn't take anybody seeing him like this and Charlie was trying to protect his privacy. The only reason I'm telling you now is because I know you need closure and I wanted you to know that wherever you son is, Dixie couldn't possibly help you. He's been like this for awhile."

Wow. Even though I didn't agree with the plan, Maggie did make me look like a martyr. I

Tranny 911: Dixie's Rise

was grateful too because Emma's entire expression changed as she approached me.

"I'm so sorry, Charlie," she said in a soft voice. "It's just that I...I miss my boy so much. I don't know what I'm going to do if..."

"I understand, Emma," I said cutting her off. I just wanted her out of my house. "And if I find out any information about Fergie I promise to let you know."

Emma looked down at the floor and back up at me. "Can you forgive me for busting into your home and forcing you to betray your friend?"

"Of course I do."

"You don't know what that means to me." She exhaled. "I don't know where my son is but before I saw you in the restaurant that day I'd given up all hope. But now things are different. I'm going to find him no matter what I have to do. I put that on what's left of my life."

SHAY HUNTER

CHAPTER NINE

Charlie

I was in a motel after just completing two appointments. I had just stuck the last cotton ball on the ass cheek of one of the Gray twins. They were beautiful tranny's that recently had gender reassignment surgeries and I was jealous. When they were lying face down on the bed to get their injections I tried to look between their legs to check out their new pussies. I did see Karen's lips and they were perfect. Whoever her surgeon was did a good job.

It wasn't that I couldn't afford the procedure. My reason for not doing it had more to do with Luke than money. Although he claimed that he would stand by my side no matter what, I got the impression that he didn't want me tampering with my body. He liked me just the way I was. I guess it shouldn't have mattered since we weren't to-gether anymore. I hated that he still influenced my decisions.

"Damn, Charlie," Karen said as she observed her ass in the mirror when I was done. Although it was littered with cotton balls to keep the crazy glue in place, you could still see the form. "You really out did yourself this time."

"She out does herself all the time," Melinda said as she slid slowly into her sweatpants.

"Y'all are so sweet," I said packing my bag. "I do what I must. Just make sure y'all continue to refer people. But only people you trust."

"We know the rules," Karen grinned. "I swear when Kenny died I was worried that we wouldn't find anybody as good as him. But I'll be damned if you didn't end up being better."

"Why would you say some shit like that?" Melinda asked her. "You act like she didn't love Kenny."

Karen immediately looked remorseful. "I'm so sorry, Charlie. I didn't mean to be insensitive. I know how much you loved Kenny and how much he cared about you. I was just stating the facts. People in DC say your work is like Picasso and I didn't think that was possible because Kenny was awesome. I didn't mean anything by it."

I smiled and tried not to cry. There weren't too many nights that went by without me thinking about Kenny. It wasn't because he taught me how to do this business. I couldn't care less about this shit.

When he came into my life he made me stronger. He wanted me to stick up for myself and not let anybody walk over me. It was because of his help that I realized that Dixie was a snake who should not be trusted. I wondered if he was disappointed in me for how I was keeping Dixie now.

"I don't take it disrespectfully," I said. "He was a great friend and I'm glad I could continue his legacy." I walked to the motel door. "Call me later if you have any issues."

I left the motel and walked slowly toward my car. I was in my head thinking about Kenny when Luke walked up to me. My heart started thumping around in my chest because I didn't know he was there. I caught a whiff of my favorite cologne that he wore and tried not to look into his eyes. He looked so sexy and I wanted to run away with him. I wanted to tell him it didn't matter that he cheated and that I missed him so much. But my pride kept me strong.

"So you following me now?" I asked as I walked around him to get into my car.

"You let me track you on your iPhone, remember? In case something happened to you."

I had totally forgotten until then. Had I remembered I would've tracked him and probably would have discovered that he was dealing with another woman. But I tried to give him his space and never wanted to come off as the jealous bitch. I wanted to trust him because he made me feel safc. Big mistake.

"I forgot but thanks for reminding me. I'll be sure to change that the moment I get in the house." I opened my car door and slid inside. He blocked the door to prevent me from shutting it.

"What's wrong with you, baby? Why you not answering my calls?"

"Because I don't want to talk." I looked at the steering wheel instead of focusing on his eyes.

"Baby, this shit is killing me. You killing us. Can you actually say that you don't miss me? We planned our lives together, Charlie. Give me a chance to explain what happened before you cut me off." He got on his knees. "I'm begging you. I'm dying."

When I looked behind him I saw the Gray twins with their hands over their mouths. I'm sure everyone knew how Luke played me and I was not going to be the fool.

"Luke, the only thing I want to say to you is if you can't claim me in public you can't claim me at all." I pushed him away, slammed my car door and pulled off, crying the entire way.

I was sitting on Belize's sofa drinking tea spiked with lots of Hennessy. She was sitting on the recliner across from me with her jaw hung as I told her the story of my life. I had been avoiding her so she didn't get the Tea. Now she had it.

"Honey, I know you're going to tell me to mind my business but—"

"You're going to get into my business anyway," I said cutting her off.

"I wouldn't be me if I didn't pry a little, Charlie. I don't know what's going on because you're giving me a little info at a time but I know for a fact that Luke is a good man. If you can't see that then you're blind, dumb and stupid."

"Thanks for the words of encouragement."

"I'm serious, Charlie. You just said that man got on his knees in the middle of the street for you. Are you really trying to say he doesn't love you? If he doesn't want you why not just let you go? Don't let him get away!"

"Why do people keep telling me that? If he's such a good man why am I sitting over here with a broken heart? Huh? And if he's so good why would he take another bitch to church to meet his mother? A real woman at that? How am I going to compete with her?"

She sighed and leaned back into the seat. "Listen, I don't know what Luke was thinking about when he took her to church but I do know that men make mistakes, Charlie. And if you want to have true love you have to learn to forgive."

"It hurts too bad, B. As much as I love him I always knew he was capable of some shit like that. And to hear it from Monday's hating ass was so embarrassing. I was about to marry this nigga and what would he have done? Left me for her? You know what, maybe this is my fault because of what I've done."

SHAY HUNTER

"This isn't your fault," Belize sighed. "So don't blame yourself. As much as I like Luke for you I'm not about to let you put that shit in your mind and on your heart."

"I'm serious, Belize. I'm doing something terrible and maybe God is punishing me for it by taking my man."

"What are you talking about?"

"I...I'm keeping Dixie paralyzed on purpose."

Her eyes widened as I continued to tell her the story from the beginning to the end. I even told her how Maggie called me on my shit. I could see the disappointment spread all over her face and I felt horrible. At the time I did it because Dixie was dangerous but now I was afraid of what might happen if he was able to walk again. I explained everything except the fact that we both killed people in injection procedures and covered for one another. Although in my situation my client died right away. We still had time to help Fergie but Dixie didn't want to.

Belize got up from the recliner and sat next to me. She placed her warm hand on my leg. "I knew something was up when I looked in Dixie's eyes. I felt it in my heart."

Tranny 911: Dixie's Rise

"I don't need that right now," I sighed.

"Hold up, hear me out. You were wrong but you can still make this right. You know you can't keep him that way. You know you have to let him go, right?"

"It's not that easy. What will prevent him from going to the police?"

"That's a chance you'll have to take but it is wrong that you're keeping him like that, baby. Don't you see that? You might as well kill him."

"Don't think I haven't thought about it."

"Charlie!"

"I'm serious," I yelled. "I haven't told you everything because it's too much. Just know that he is not an angel and he could've hurt a lot of people. I'm saving lives by keeping him that way."

"Charlie," she said softly, "if you don't let him go things will get worse for you. I promise. You playing God and you not him. What you are is a good person and you have a heart. Don't let Dixie take that from you. Let...him...go."

CHAPTER TEN

Charlie

I was swinging my hips on the dance floor at Club Wiggles thinking about one thing...that I couldn't remember the last time I'd been this drunk. The bright, colorful disco ball on the ceiling shined against me and I kept looking at my silhouette in the mirror. If Luke saw me he would probably lose his mind. More and more everyday, I was starting to look like the woman I always wanted to be.

Every now and again I'd take a sip of my apple martini that sat on the bar and I'd see a few Judy's looking over at me. Some of them were jealous because I looked so much like a woman but my closest friends were happy for me. I could tell when I looked into their eyes.

I'd just left the bar and was on my way back to the dance floor again when someone grabbed my hand. At first I thought it was Belize telling me to slow down like she had been all night but when I turned around and saw a handsome stranger I was pleasantly surprised.

He wasn't as tall as Luke or tatted up like him, but he was still attractive. His copper colored skin seemed to glow under the light and I loved how neat he kept his five o'clock shadow.

"You know it's rude to touch a girl without her permission, right?" I asked hoping he'd come back with a sexy reply.

"I wouldn't know anything about that because I only deal with women."

I like. I thought to myself. *I like a lot.*

"Before you go back on that dance floor and drive me crazy, let me buy you another drink. I want to see if you talk as smoothly as you dance."

"I talk smoother," I said. "But I think I've had too much already. I appreciate the offer though."

"Then let me get you some ginger ale." He smiled. "I promise, I won't take too much of your time. I just want to know the woman behind those moves. That's it and that's all."

SHAY HUNTER

I was lonely so I decided to stay at the bar for a few minutes. Besides this was probably what I wanted all along. Attention from a man I found attractive. Luke fucked my head up and I needed to know that I still had it since it was obvious that I was back on the market.

"My name is Dean," he said. "What's yours?"

"Charlie. And let me be clear, I'm trans-."

"I know what you are and you're still sexy as hell."

"Thank you," I responded trying not to blush. "So tell me something about yourself." I took a seat next to him at the bar. His light brown eyes drove me crazy.

"You mean outside of the fact that I've been staring at you all night? And outside of the fact that I told my friends to get lost so that I could have a chance to just kick it with you for a few minutes?"

I giggled. "Yeah, something different."

"Well I'm a single man in need of some companionship. I was in the army for five years and I was just honorably discharged a few months ago. I was too busy when I was in the service to think about a relationship but now I'm not. So tell me something about yourself."

I started to tell him that I was engaged but I left the ring at home after I caught Luke cheating. "I'm newly single and just mingling. That's all you need to know for now."

"So you aren't looking for anything serious?"

"I don't know what I'm looking for. Right now I just want to have fun, you know? If something happens then so be it." When I felt my lower stomach bubble I realized I had to go pee. "I'm going to the bathroom. I'll be right back."

Without waiting on his reply I dipped into the ladies restroom. I rushed into a stall, unzipped my pants and released my penis. As the urine released itself from my body and splashed into the toilet while I was standing up I thought about the day when I wouldn't have to use the bathroom this way. After my surgery I could sit on the toilet like a real girl, without my penis brushing against the diseased water inside of the nasty bowl. I wondered if Luke would love me more then.

You know what, fuck Luke! It's all about me now!

SHAY HUNTER

I was just about to pull up my pants when the stall door came flying open. Suddenly I was looking into Dean's brown eyes. I started to curse him out but I could tell that he wanted me. He pushed me against the stall's wall and pressed his warm tongue into my mouth. I've kissed men before and their kisses were always animalistic. His was slow and passionate and it made me pull him closer toward my warm body. In a drunken haze, for the moment anyway, I felt like I was in love.

After he kissed me I just knew he was about to turn me around and try to fuck me, instead he placed tiny kisses all the way from my ear to my neck. I was so horny now that my dick pressed against his stiffness and for a moment I felt like a man, which was always a turn off. That is until he whispered, "You're so beautiful."

I immediately relaxed and allowed him to do whatever he wanted to my body. It wasn't difficult because his touch was gentle and he was nothing like the tricks in the past who fucked me, and then beat me up the next minute and told me all the reasons it was my fault for them being gay. Dean treated me like I belonged to him and I wanted to go to the next level.

I turned around and allowed my pants to fall at my ankles. I just knew in any minute that he would be barreling inside of my body. Instead he leaned over my shoulder and asked, "Are you sure?"

Wow! A real man! Where did he come from? Maybe it was the fact that he was a military man but he was kind and gentle.

"Yes. I'm sure," I moaned.

A minute later he was pushing himself inside of me and it felt so right. I pushed back into him so that I could feel his stiffness deep inside my body. I wasn't aware that I was crying until I saw one of my tears splash against my dick as I stroked it. This was wrong but it felt so right.

Dean continued to grab at my waist and move in and out of me. When I heard him moan like he couldn't hold it anymore I stroked myself harder until my cream splashed into my hand. The moment of pleasure only lasted a second before I realized what I had done... I'd just had unprotected sex in the bathroom at Club Wiggles.

"I'm sorry for treating you like this," Dean said softly. "I was hoping we could talk but when you said you were going to the bathroom I figured

SHAY HUNTER

it was my cue to come in behind you. I'm sorry if I was being presumptuous."

Wow. Also a first. Dean was not only attractive but he was also a gentleman and I couldn't hurt him by making him think it was anything but sex. This time I was the one who only wanted one thing. Besides, my heart belonged to another.

I grabbed some tissue out of the dispenser and wiped my hand. I dropped it on the floor and pulled my pants up. We both stood in the stall in a huge awkward moment of silence. I couldn't face him because I knew what I was about to say.

"I'm sorry, Dean," I said looking down at the floor. "But I'm not looking for anything but this." I bravely looked into his eyes to give him the respect I would've wanted someone to give me back in the day.

He looked disappointed. "Give me a chance. Nobody is saying we have to move in together or anything. But I like you and I think you like me. So what's wrong with that?"

"Everything. Sadly enough, I'm in love," I said as I opened the stall's door and walked out.

Tranny 911: Dixie's Rise

CHAPTER ELEVEN

Charlie

I sped down the street thinking about what I'd just done at Club Wiggles. Since I'd been with Luke I had been faithful, never thinking about another man and yet I'd just had unprotected sex in the women's bathroom like some sorority slut.

Tears poured down my cheek and I wiped them away roughly. Although Luke and I were not together I still felt like I violated his trust and his love. I hated the power he had over me.

I was about five miles from my house when my cell phone rang. To get my mind off of Dean and Luke I reluctantly answered. "Hello."

"Are you crazy or just dumb?" Belize asked me with an attitude.

"What are you talking about now?" I sighed.

SHAY HUNTER

"Everybody is talking about how you just fucked Dirty Dick Dean in the bathroom and shit. Please say it's not true. Please say you didn't give your cookies to the first monster who wanted a bite."

"Dirty Dick Dean?" I screamed with my eyes widening. This dude had a moniker?

"Yes, Charlie. That nigga is married and all he does is come down to the club, grab a faggy flavor of his choice, take her in the bathroom and cry love while he's busting her back out. Half of the time the nigga don't even wear condoms. I wouldn't be surprised if you caught something. What the hell is wrong with you?"

My heart thumped wildly in my chest. Not only did I not see him being married, he was nasty too. This was too much. "I can't talk right now, Belize. I really have to call you back."

"I'm not getting off of the phone with you and you're going to listen to me this time, bitch! Now I know you're fucked up about what's going on with Luke. I get that. But you aren't one of those girls, Charlie. Between this shit with Dean and what's going on with Dixie and Luke you out of touch with reality. And I suggest that you take the time to figure out where you're going with your life. You're better than all this shit."

"Who the fuck are you?" I yelled. "Huh? Are you so much better than me just because I fucked a lame in the bathroom? I'm tired of you fussing at me and making me feel like a child! You may be Mommy Dearest but you not mine!" I pressed the end button in her ear.

A few seconds later the phone rang again and I reluctantly answered. "Hello," I sighed knowing who it was.

"I love you, bitch, and I'll call you tomorrow," Belize said before hanging up on me.

Despite everything that was going on I couldn't help but smile. It reminded me why Belize was my closest friend. She gave good advice but she didn't take me too seriously when I got mad and right now I needed that shit.

When I got to the house I knew the first thing I wanted to do was take a shower. I had to get Dean's stink off my body. I parked the car, grabbed my purse and walked inside my house. I headed straight for the bathroom because I didn't want to go anywhere near my bed.

Once inside the bathroom I pulled my clothes off and threw them in the laundry basket.

SHAY HUNTER

Then I reached under the sink and grabbed a disposable douche. I opened the packaging, sat on the toilet and plunged the syringe into my asshole. I pressed the liquid until it drained out.

When I was done I ran the hot water in the shower and reached under the sink to grab the bleach. I stepped into the tub with the bleach and poured some of it on my washcloth. I washed my body as hard as I could with bleach before wiping my butt too. It burned like hell but I deserved it. This was one of the worst nights of my life.

"What you crying for?" I heard someone say.

I stopped moving and cut the water off. "Is that you, Maggie?"

"No," the person said flatly. "It's not Nurse Aggy."

The alcohol was still in my system so it took me a minute to realize what was happening. I had to be dreaming. This could not be happening. I must be dead or in hell because this person can't talk. He can't!

I opened the yellow curtain slowly and stared into Dixie's evil eyes. How was he standing there? How was he standing period?

"You look like you saw a ghost, Charlie," he laughed.

Tranny 911: *Dixie's Rise*

"Dixie...I..."

"Let me stop you there, bitch. Ain't no need in you lying or telling me that you didn't mean to keep me paralyzed. You told me that over and over again when you walked into my room. You're awful." He stepped toward me. "You're worse than me even. And I'm going to return the favor, Charlie." He took another step closer. "I'm going to make your life a living hell."

He pulled a bat from behind his back and knocked me over the head. My chin hit the tub and I passed out.

SHAY HUNTER

CHAPTER TWELVE

Dixie

Nurse Aggy's tiny studio apartment in DC was much smaller than I envisioned. I couldn't see how an adult could live there and not feel like and infant sleeping in a crib.

You step out of her bedroom area and you're in the kitchen; you walk out of the kitchen and you're in the bathroom. There was no privacy and no place to store even your smallest thoughts. Even though it was tight, I had to give her credit; she had her place clean and in order. Everything had its place and the aroma of cinnamon and vanilla filled the air.

I sat on the edge of her bed holding a cup of hot tea. I kept looking at my fingers because after months I actually regained the use of my hands. I had access to my body for about a month before I left the house but I couldn't leave. Nurse Aggy wanted to make sure I was completely strong before we made an escape. I guess she was concerned with Charlie running up on us and knew she couldn't carry my weight if he caught us and tried to kill us.

To be sure I was in shape, Nurse Aggy would walk me around the room when Charlie wasn't there and showed me how to use my limbs all over again. At first everything was stiff and even now my back hurt from not moving it for months.

If Charlie realized that I could walk on the day Emma came to the house to talk, he would probably die. I wanted so badly to choke Charlie but I held myself together. Plus it was important to Nurse Aggy that I play it smart, and I did.

The funny thing about the situation is this; Charlie probably believed that just because I hit him over the top of the head with a bat in the bathroom I was done with him. He had no idea that in my mind killing him would be far too easy after what he did to me.

SHAY HUNTER

I used to wish for death when I was lying in the bed paralyzed but over time I learned patience, a trait that I never bothered myself with before.

Nurse Aggy had no idea that I had bigger plans for Charlie. In her mind I was going to go to the cops in the morning and explain everything that happened to me. She was wrong and she would soon find out.

"How do you feel?" Nurse Aggy asked sitting next to me on the bed. "In any pain?"

I was dressed in a pair of baggy grey sweatpants and a long black t-shirt that belonged to her ex-boyfriend/stepdad. She brought the clothes to me when we were plotting my escape.

"I'm fine I guess," I said sitting the cup down. "I just have a lot to do and I don't even know where to start."

"Try not to do too much, Dixon," she said looking into my eyes. "You've been in a bed for almost two years. The last thing you need to be doing is—"

For some reason I was overcome with anger at that moment. I rubbed my throbbing temples because I didn't want to say what was about to come out of my mouth in the wrong way. I was trying to use the patience shit I developed over time but I must say it was very difficult.

"Why do you do that?" I asked looking into her eyes, interrupting her thought. "Huh?"

"Do what?"

"Tell me what I should be doing?" I turned around so that my body faced hers. "You did that shit for years and in all that time the only thing I was thinking was what I would say to you if I ever got the chance. And now I have it."

She leaned back a little. "I never knew you felt that way. What did you want to tell me?"

"To shut the fuck up," I screamed in her face. "Nobody's the boss of me. Nobody!"

She stood up and backed against the wall. She looked as if she had allowed a serial killer into her home. Maybe she had. Clearing her throat she said, "I'm sorry, Dixon. I'm just worried about you that's all. And I want to take care of you so that you will be alright."

I was suddenly intrigued. Despite my attitude, she still wanted to help me and that made her interesting. "Do you really want to take care of me?"

She stepped closer. "More than anything."

SHAY HUNTER

I stood up and dropped my sweats and underwear. They rested at my ankles and I sat on the edge of the bed with my legs hanging open. I stroked my stiff penis until it was so hard I thought the blood would explode out of my skin. "Then come take care of me right. It's been a long time and I need a fix."

She didn't waste any time dropping to her knees and crawling toward me. I knew this was what she always wanted.

In a second flat, my dick was stuffed in her mouth and pressing against her windpipe. I pulled the hideous brown wig off her head and tossed it on the floor so that I could feel her scalp.

Yeah, this was nice. Now I was face fucking a man, which was just the way I liked it.

I was surprised too. Nurse Aggy had skills and was better than I imagined. Her mouth was warm and she was making it sloppy wet. No wonder her stepfather was coming over here and lacing her up. The girl could suck a dick better than a plunger sucked out shit in a toilet.

I was just about to cum when I pressed all of my weight onto the back of her head so that my cum would shoot down her throat. She was gagging and throwing up on my dick trying to get some air but I wouldn't let her go. When I finally released my semen into her mouth, I liberated her. She fell backwards and held her neck.

"Why did you do that?" she asked with wide eyes. "I couldn't breathe."

"I'm sorry," I said trying to catch my breath. "That shit was feeling so good that I couldn't help myself." I wiped the sweat off my brow. "Come here though."

She crawled toward me and stood on her knees between my legs. For a second she looked like a helpless boy/child and I was her deranged father.

"I appreciate everything you've done for me, Maggie, by helping me walk again and shit like that. Nobody else would've done the things you did for me. For whatever reason, people generally don't like me but you're different."

She smiled.

I ran my hand down the sides of her face and then her neck. I wanted to feel how such a small throat could take such a big dick. I knew I was larger than the average man because when I was in high school I made a girl named Eleanor suck my dick for forty minutes straight in the boy's locker room. She passed out twice because her airway was blocked and I had to revive her to prevent a murder charge.

Once I had Nurse Aggy's throat in my hand something came over me. Its slenderness reminded me of Charlie's neck so I begin to squeeze it lightly.

"What are you doing?" Nurse Aggy asked as she tried to slide away from me.

My hold grew tighter and she attempted to move back but I wouldn't let her get away. I was in control. Besides I was well now and hadn't killed in months. So I overpowered her and pressed my weight on top of her body as she lay under me on the floor. With outstretched arms I squeezed her throat harder. She tried to fight me by slapping at my arms and scratching the flesh of my skin but she was no match. I squashed her windpipe so hard that her eyes rolled to the back of her head.

Now she looked beautiful.

Silent and dead.

Just the way I liked it.

I stood up and I walked toward her ugly purple purse on the dresser and grabbed her wallet. I took the two hundred bucks she had inside and her bankcard. I knew the pass code because she gave it to me earlier when we went to 7-Eleven. I was at the ATM and she told me whatever she had was mine and she didn't want any secrets between us. I wondered if she would feel that same way if she was alive.

With the money in my pocket I decided it was time to pursue the dream I had ever since I could move again. I picked the phone up on the wall, dialed *69 and called Charlie's cell phone. Just as I thought, he answered.

"Hello," he said in a shaky voice.

"Enjoy your life for as long as you have it because you and I both know that everything you have, and everything you own belongs to me. And I'm coming for it."

SHAY HUNTER

CHAPTER THIRTEEN

Charlie

I was in the dressing room at Club Wiggles doing Kenya's makeup for a show she had that night with her partner. Kenya is a six foot three inch tall tranny that doesn't look anything like a woman unless I beat her face. I was trying to stay focused but I didn't want to be there and I couldn't go home either. I had been living with Belize ever since Dixie tried to kill me a week ago and my life was a wreck.

I had just finished placing Kenya's last eyelash on when I stepped back and looked at my work. It wasn't bad but I had done better. "I'm finished. Tell me if you like it or not. It's okay if you don't because I can do it over."

Kenya spun around in the salon chair and looked at herself in the lighted mirror. "Oooo,

Miss Charlie, I do declare that there ain't a makeup artist in the world who could touch your work." She placed both hands on her face and stood up. "Why, child, you have made me as beautiful as the Queen Beyoncé herself."

I thought her comment was going a little too far but I didn't let her know.

She ran her hands down her sparkling gold dress and turned from left to right to examine her curves. Last year I did her butt injections so she probably was on cloud nine now.

Although Kenya wasn't better looking than her best friend, Goldie, who was also a tranny, she sure did light up when she was on stage and it was always a treat to watch her shows. She never resembled any of the singers she tried to imitate but at some point, maybe around the first minute, she became them. She embodied everything they represented and it was always a sight to see.

"Just look at my hair," she said running her hands through the cascading black full lace wig I glued and curled on her head. "I just can't get over your skills." She looked at me as if I wasn't real. "Who are you really? Picasso reincarnated?"

I was about to say thank you when Goldie came in the dressing room with a red dress that

SHAY HUNTER

matched Kenya's. They were doing a Destiny
Child's number that evening for the show and although there were three members in the group,
they said Miss Michelle didn't require a singer
and wasn't a factor.

Despite Goldie's face being beat to the gods,
because I had done it earlier, her head was covered with a tan wig cap. When she looked up at
Kenya's head she was beyond angry.

"Bitch, I knew you were born with one ball
but I had no idea you were crazy too," she yelled
at Kenya. "I have been looking all over for my
wig."

"Get out of my face, child," Kenya said sitting down in the chair. "My audience awaits and I
don't need to hear your lips flapping right now."

"Get out of your face? Bitch, you are wearing Goldie's customized Gilda," she said placing
her hand over her chest. She went to pull the wig
but it didn't budge. I had glued it on that good.

Kenya turned around in the chair, looked up
to Goldie in the mirror and laughed. "Sorry, honey. But Miss Charlie laid this Gilda and it's not
going anywhere."

The two of them took to yelling and scream-
ing and somewhere, amongst all of the arguing, I

burst into tears. My life had become such a mess and the more I thought about it the more I realized that it was all my fault. I backed up into the wall and my body slumped to the floor. My ass rested on a size thirteen pump and I pulled my knees toward my body and cried even harder.

Kenya and Goldie stopped yelling and looked at me. "Oh Miss Charlie, please don't cry," Kenya said in a soft motherly tone. She looked up at Goldie. "Do you see what you've done? You've gotten the child upset."

"I'm so sorry, Charlie. You see, me and Kenya going to be alright and there ain't no reason you should take that to heart. I have many more full lace wigs in my trunk and can grab another if need be."

"That ain't it," I sobbed while looking up at them. "It's about Dixie."

"What about that fossil faced queen?" Kenya asked placing her hands on her hips.

Both of their faces contorted at the mere mentioning of her name. Dixie didn't have any fans around here because of her selfish antics. She would do things like steal tips from other trannies while they performed on the stage and she even

slept with their tricks for less money. She was no-
torious and nobody liked her.

"I did something so awful," I said wiping the
falling tears from my face. "Something I can't
take back although I wish I could."

"What is it?" Goldie asked as they both sat
down.

"Don't tell 'em," Belize said entering the
dressing room. She looked beautiful too. She was
wearing a natural looking black lace front wig and
it was pulled back into a sassy ponytail. She
tossed her red bag on the dressing room table and
strutted toward me. "You keep your mouth closed,
you hear me?"

"Shut up, monkey fish," Kenya yelled at her.
"We were having a private conversation with this
child before you stomped in here."

"In the first place, bitch, I never stomp anywhere. I simply glide with grace and elegance."
Belize yelled reading Kenya. "And furthermore, I
am in charge of this child and you don't—"

"It's okay," I said loudly. "I don't mind telling them what happened."

Belize sat on the dresser and folded her arms
in front of her. She shook her head in disappointment and said, "Well, go ahead if you must. If you

want your business broadcasted throughout Club Wiggles like it's the Washington Post you go right ahead."

Unmoved by her threats, I went on to tell them almost everything, minus the murders and the burial of the bodies of course. When I was done Kenya and Goldie's mouths hung open.

"I only see one problem with this scenario," Kenya said sitting back in the seat and crossing her legs.

"And what's that?" I asked.

"You should've killed that hag instead of letting it survive," she proclaimed. "Had you done that you would've put the entire world out of misery and I doubt a jury on this planet would've convicted you."

"Why would you tell this child some shit like that?" Belize interjected. "This is why I didn't want her telling y'all because you don't have the good common sense your father's cum gave you."

"But wait, Belize," Goldie added. "Miss. Kenya is many things but in this instance she's right. That thing of a monster deserves nothing short of death. I mean think about it for a minute. Had she got rid of her she wouldn't be in fear for her life."

SHAY HUNTER

Belize walked over to me and bent down. "This is why I wanted you to keep this private until we thought of a better plan. I know it feels good to have them tell you that you were justified in your actions but you know it's not true. And I'm not here to tell you that you were all the way wrong either."

"I already know what you're about to say, B."

"No you don't but I want you to know you are better than what Dixie is trying to make you out to be. And we are going to take some time to figure out a plan so that she'll get what she deserves. All I'm asking is that you be smart."

"I don't know about all that but I will say this," Kenya added. "Even the devil has to go back to the hell he crawled out of eventually. And I suggest you help him get there."

CHAPTER FOURTEEN

Charlie

I was cruising in my car after just coming back from the STD Clinic. What a fucking day! After having sex with Dirty Dick Dean I knew I had to check myself out. If I was going to start my life over and be with someone who wanted me, I needed to make sure I was in the best of health.

After leaving the clinic I had one more important thing to do. I had to stop back at the house I shared with Dixie and get my important papers. I hadn't been back since Dixie hit me and I didn't want to go now. The choice wasn't mine. Everything I owned was there.

I was about five miles from the house when my phone rang. I hit the Bluetooth button to activate the speakers. "Hello."

"Hi, is this Charlie?" a soft voice asked.

I couldn't tell if the person was a tranny or a fish but I knew I didn't know them personally. "Who is this? And how did you get my number?"

"I'm sorry if I'm bothering you. And I know this is not allowed but I paid Monday five hundred dollars for your number. I would've paid more if she had asked because this is so important."

I sighed. Monday was getting on my fucking nerves. "What do you mean you paid Monday?"

"I have been looking for someone reputable to do my injections but I couldn't find anybody. Monday is a friend of my cousin's and I saw her body transform. I want the same thing."

"I don't know what you're talking about."

"Please, Charlie. I need this bad because the chicks at the strip club I work at are running rings around me and I got a little boy to take care of. If it's money you want I can get it. I have a savings account my mother set up for my son's college education before she died. You can have it if you want. I'll pay you double if you just give me an appointment. That's all I'm asking."

Wow. I couldn't believe whoever this was would stoop so low. "Listen, I can't talk right now. If you really want an appointment let me call you back, okay?"

"Thank you so much, Charlie," she said relieved, as if I had said yes already.

When I got off of the phone with her she texted me her number like she said she would. I didn't know if I would do her work yet because I didn't trust new clients, but I knew I wasn't going to charge her extra if I did. Taking a baby's college fund was not my cup of tea and I wasn't hard pressed for cash.

When I got to my house and pulled up in front I took a moment to look at the property. My plan was simple—run inside, grab what I needed and run back out. So I parked my car on the curb and approached the house cautiously. I checked my surroundings to be sure I wasn't walking into an ambush.

Earlier that day, Belize begged me not to go until she was with me but she didn't get off of work until later that evening and I didn't want to wait that long.

When I didn't see any strange cars parked out front of the house I took the key out of my purse and walked inside. I closed and locked the door behind me and the moment I took three steps I could feel something was off.

Concerned for my life I pulled the gun that Belize gave me out of my purse. She blessed it for me and called it the God Gun because it would do His work if need be.

"If you're in here I'm going to kill you dead," I said aiming in the house. "I'm not fucking around with you."

"I really hope you won't kill me," I heard someone say although I couldn't see him yet due to the wall that hid the living room. It didn't matter though, because I knew who it was. "Not when I have so much left to say to you."

A few seconds later Luke stepped in front of me and I lowered my weapon. The last thing I wanted was to shoot him by accident. "How did you know I was here?"

"Belize called me. She wouldn't give me the details, but she said something was wrong and she wanted me to be here to protect you." He raised his arms. "So I let myself in through the window in the back."

He was wearing blue jeans, a fresh black t-shirt and he looked so fucking sexy. Damn I loved that man.

I placed the gun in my purse. "I should call the police on your ass for breaking and entering."

"I'm hoping you won't do that."

"Where is your car?" I asked trying to appear angry even though I missed him more than I did a relationship with my parents.

"I hid it down the block because I knew you wouldn't come inside if you saw it. It took me five minutes to walk up here but here I am."

"I can't believe Belize did that shit," I said shaking my head. "For the life of me I can't understand why she won't just mind her own business."

"Don't be mad at her, Charlie." He stepped closer and I could smell his cologne and my knees weakened. "She really cares about you. And I don't know what's going on, but she thought enough of you to call me, knowing full well how angry you would be."

"I can't deal with this right now," I admitted as I walked around him toward my room.

He softly grabbed my hand and then got on his knees. He looked up at me. "Charlie, I can't live without you, baby. And I know things looked bad when you walked up on me at church but if you would give me a chance to explain, I believe in my heart that I can clear everything up."

Why was he doing this to me? Why couldn't he just leave me alone?

"Luke, I can't deal with this shit right now."

"I know, baby," he said as a tear rolled down his face. "I know, but I believe whatever you have going on would be easier if you had love in your life. You deserve happiness. You deserve me and I deserve you."

"Get up, Luke."

"Not until you tell me you'll take me back."

I looked down at him and in that moment knew that he was mine. All mine. I had wasted so much time on a chick who was obviously not in his heart enough to prevent him from crying back to me.

Fuck that bitch.

Fuck the world.

So I said, "Okay."

His eyes widened. "Okay?" He repeated.

"I said okay, but on two conditions."

"Anything."

"That you first stand up."

"What else? Understand that I would do anything for you."

Tranny 911: *Dixie's Rise*

"The second thing I want is for you to let me live with you."

His eyes expanded and he pulled me forcefully toward his hard body. He had wanted me to move in with him for years and finally I said yes. My reasons were twofold. First, I really wanted to be with him and secondly, I couldn't live here anymore.

"Of course you can live with me, baby. My home has always been yours. You don't know what you just did for my heart but I have all intentions on showing you in time."

This felt so right but there was one problem. I slept with another man and wasn't sure what impact that would have on our bond.

SHAY HUNTER

CHAPTER FIFTEEN

Charlie

I was inside Bells & Whistles wedding store with a frustrated Belize. She stood in front of a white female clerk with my dress draped over her arm as she continued to read her for blood. "Why is it that whenever I come here and request a certain thing, you give me another? Are you dumb, slow or all the above?"

"Belize, what are you talking about?" she asked as her face turned a deeper red hue. "I took the neckline down and placed the pearl beads on the sleeves just as you asked. What more do you want?"

"I also told you to bring it in a little more in the waist, remember? We had Charlie in here for over an hour while you measured her. What was all of that for if not for the dress alterations? Huh?"

The clerk didn't respond. Instead, she poked out her lips out and rolled her eyes.

"Don't go mums on me now," Belize continued. "Not after you had so much to say earlier."

The clerk snatched the dress off of Belize's arm. "I'll take care of it." She stormed away.

Belize was about to run behind her, probably to snatch the brunette hair from her scalp but I stopped her just in time with a soft hand on her shoulder. "Calm down, B. It's not that deep."

"Yes it is," she yelled at me as if it were her wedding she was planning. "This will be the first wedding in our circle and I want it perfect."

"And it will be," I reassured her.

"Can you believe it?" her face softened and she appeared to go elsewhere in her mind. "The *very* first. Before you, we didn't think it was possible to marry someone we loved and now it's happening. Your wedding gives girls like me hope and I don't want this event to be just another day. I want it spectacular." She looked down at the floor. "I care about you so much, Charlie."

When I looked into her eyes I could see the love she had for me. Belize really wanted the best for me and it was written all over her face. "It will be great," I smiled. "And I'm so happy you are in my life. You helped me through a lot recently and I am so blessed." I hugged her tightly before letting her go.

We walked over to a daybed and sat down in front of a large, beautiful window. Belize grabbed the small white binder that sat next to her on the brass table that she used to record all of my details. After updating me on the major items, she flipped through the book again.

"First off, are you sure you should be putting everything in that book?" I asked looking down at it. "What if it's lost?"

"I'm a old school bitch, Charlie. I don't keep things in my phone and shit like that. It's so impersonal. And the only time this book hasn't been in my possession is when you asked to borrow it for the numbers you needed."

I didn't feel like arguing with her so I said, "Forget all that. Why did you change the place we are having our reception without running it past me first? I really liked the first venue, Belize."

"Are you serious?" she asked lowering her head. "Or have you forgotten that we have a crisis on our hands?"

Tranny 911: Dixie's Rise

"I haven't forgotten about Dixie but that was the perfect spot."

"It may have been but I don't want him popping up ruining it all."

"But why didn't you tell me?"

"I didn't tell you that I changed it because you and Luke had been sewn at the hips. And when I called you to give you the details you told me to kick rocks and to do what I wanted. So I did."

I laughed because she was telling the truth.

"And don't worry about the venue because the one I found is better. Trust me. If I know one thing it's how to throw a gala." She grew silent and looked over me. "You look so happy since you've been back with Luke, Charlie. Like life has gotten into you and given you another breath."

"I am happy. Waking up to that man every day has reminded me how much I missed him in my life. I wasn't living before he came back to me and as mad as I was that you got into my business by telling him to come to the house, I'm also glad you did."

"I must admit, I was hoping that my little betrayal would bring you both back together but I couldn't be sure." She grew silent again. "But, baby, I've been thinking about something else. Have you gotten tested?"

"Of course," I said remembering my tryst with Dirty Dick Dean. "I couldn't live with myself if I didn't."

"I'm not trying to get into your love life but are you—"

"I'm not having sex with him, B," I interrupted. "I told him that I wanted to save our moment for when we got married. He's just happy to have me living with him for now so he doesn't press the issue."

"When do you get the results back?"

"In a few weeks," I sighed. "I'm really hoping things will be okay."

She ran the back of her hand down the side of my face. "Things will work out."

"Why you ask about Dean anyway?"

She exhaled. "I got word that he gave his wife HIV. She had to be taken to a mental institution because she lost it when she found out. A few queens he fucked are getting tested and I wanted to make sure you were too."

I placed my hand over my heart to stop it from beating so rapidly. Then I stood up and

Tranny 911: *Dixie's Rise*

paced the small area in front of where we sat. "What…what do you mean he has HIV?"

"He's supposedly positive, Charlie. But you can't believe everything you hear in Club Wiggles. I'm just letting you know because you're my friend. But as always you've already taken the necessary precautions and that's all you can do. Now I know that you're worried but even if he's positive there's still a chance that you aren't. Let's pray for the best."

I felt like I was hyperventilating and I tried to calm down. "I hope you're right because if I am positive, I can't marry Luke. I would never want to ruin his life like that."

"Now you're moving too fast with all that crazy talk," Belize said. "Hush, child, and let's talk about something else. What's going on with Dixie?"

"Things are quiet," I sighed. "Too quiet. After he left me in the bathroom to die, he called me later and said that he would ruin my life. He hasn't shown back up and I don't know what he means. He could've killed me right then but he didn't and that scares me even more."

"Maybe he's gone, Charlie. Maybe he realizes that what you did to him he had coming."

SHAY HUNTER

"No," I said shaking my head. "He's waiting for the perfect time." I looked out of the large window. "And when it happens I just hope that I'm prepared."

CHAPTER SIXTEEN

Dixie

I stood across the street from Bells & Whistles smoking a cigarette. I'd been standing there for hours doing what I normally do, checking out Charlie and her daily routine.

Look at that bitch standing in front of the window as if she's queen. And that ratchet Belize ain't nothing but Charlie's chambermaid, at her beck and call to do whatever she wants when she wants. I hate both of them bitches but it's Charlie who keeps me up at night.

After I took Nurse Aggy's body out of her apartment and threw her into the trunk of her car, I dumped her in the Anacostia River in Washington DC. I knew she would never be seen again because the city didn't care about that river or its secrets.

When I was done I drove back to her apartment and created a plan. I needed a clear one that would allow me to take everything from Charlie that he loved the most. And if my details were right, and things went my way, Charlie's world would come to an end very soon.

I removed another cigarette from my jeans when a woman, who was talking on the phone, walked in my direction with a four or five year old child. The little boy was staring in my face like I was a movie and it was working my nerves. Right before he passed me he yelled, "Mommy, look at that man. He's ugly."

I looked at his mother hoping she would check his fat ass but she acted like she didn't hear him. Instead she continued to run her mouth on the phone. So when they walked past me I kicked the boy in his ass sending him straight to the ground…head first.

"Hold on, Benita," the woman said looking down at her child who was crying his eyes out. "Get your fat ass up, always falling on the ground and shit." She yanked him roughly by the arm and when he was on his feet she got back on the phone. I laughed my ass off.

Because I was fucking with them, I almost blew my cover. When I saw Charlie and Belize walk out of the store and stand in front of it, I rushed toward Nurse Aggy's white Honda and slumped down in the driver's seat so that they wouldn't see me.

Belize was holding a small book closely to her chest. They said a few words and then Charlie hugged Belize before they walked to their cars.

I slowly pulled the car out and trailed Belize. From the back I saw her dancing around in her black Ford pickup truck looking like an idiot. She was probably dancing to some old show tunes with her dried up, funky ass. I could tell by the comfort level she exhibited that she had no idea that I was following her…big mistake.

The funny thing is I didn't hate Belize. She wouldn't have been so bad if she didn't play Charlie so close. When I used to hang out at Club Wiggles I thought we were all cool, the three of us. Belize, who was my friend first, would come over my house sometimes and we would go on and on about life and men. Charlie would always be there but she was such a square Belize paid her no real attention.

Things went on in that order for a year but before long I got in a relationship with a nigga named Aaron. I went through a lot with Aaron, and when he broke my heart for another queen down Club Wiggles, Belize was there to console me.

Everybody thinks I'm so cruel, like I don't have any emotions or feelings but it's not true. I wanted to be a true friend to Belize but when I brought up an argument that Charlie and me had about rent, Belize took her side.

Charlie had gotten fired from his job after working for only two months and I was tired of pulling his weight. I told Belize that I was going to throw him out the next day and he told Charlie behind my back. Charlie ended up getting another job but I knew then that I couldn't trust Belize. We had been low-key beefing ever since.

After trailing Belize for about twenty minutes, she pulled up in the same neighborhood that she'd always lived in. I'm sure she couldn't see me because I was about five houses down from where she lived.

I had all intentions on being patient because in the past when I moved too swiftly I got myself into trouble. If there was one thing that I learned from being paralyzed it was that the things you want most in life need patience and attention.

Three hours later, darkness set on the neighborhood and I knew it was time to make my move. If I remembered correctly I'd overheard Belize talking one day about how her on-again, off-again boyfriend, Stephen, kicked her basement door in when they broke up. She said because of it if you jiggled the knob hard the door would pop open. Charlie asked Belize why she didn't get it fixed and she said because she wouldn't have to give Stephen another key if they got back together. I was hoping that this was still the case.

After waiting enough time I crept out of the car and strolled up to the house. It was a quiet neighborhood so I didn't see anybody outside to notice me. I slipped toward the back door and walked down the steps leading to the basement. Before jiggling the knob I looked around again and still didn't see anybody.

When I was ready I jiggled it harder and the door didn't budge. Fuck! Please don't tell me she got it fixed after all. Taking a deep breath, I jig-

SHAY HUNTER

gled it once more and then twice, and before I knew it I gained entrance.

I inched inside and closed the door softly behind me. I had been over Belize's house before so I knew where her bedroom was. I tiptoed through the basement and up the stairs leading to the rest of the house. It was extremely dark but I knew my way.

I was trying to be silent and since it was around midnight I figured she would be asleep anyway. I prowled toward her bedroom and from where I stood I could see her door was wide open.

Belize was on the bed, face down with her butt out. The white sheets outlined her dark body and she was snoring to the Gods. Her ass was perfect and hard just like I liked it and the light from the DVD player glowed against her chocolate skin. Because she wasn't in drag, she wasn't wearing a wig or make up. I immediately grew hard and figured I had to do something about it.

I took my stiff dick out and walked over toward the bed. I stroked my rod in my hands until it was leaking pre-cum. Staring at her ass cheeks I massaged the shaft up and down until I was tingling all over. A few seconds later my cum shot out and landed on her ass cheeks. I hadn't expected that to happen so I dropped to my knees to hide. But when she continued to snore as if I wasn't there I stood up.

When I pulled myself together I searched for the book she was carrying earlier that day. Before long, I found it on the dresser behind her and I stuffed it in my pants. I was about to leave when something came over me. Every now and again I got a murderous urge that couldn't be pacified. I believe now was that time.

I was about to choke her out when I heard a male's voice yelling, "Babe, why you leave the basement door open?"

I looked down at Belize and luckily she was still snoring. So I dipped out of the room and hung in the darkness of the hallway before the man came inside and spotted me. Moments later a tall dude passed me but he couldn't see me because I was concealed. I rushed toward the backdoor and out of the house with the book in my hands.

That was a close call and that dude, whoever he was, had just saved Belize's life.

SHAY HUNTER

CHAPTER SEVENTEEN

Charlie

The sunshine eased through the bottom of the blinds and spilled into Luke's bedroom, brightening everything inside. I was lying on my right side trying to get myself together mentally. Luke shuffled a little, yawned and then eased up behind me, kissing me softly on the neck. I smiled.

"What you thinking about, beautiful?" he asked as his breath warmed my nape.

"Us, and our future life together."

"And what else?"

"And how nice it would be if you would wear a tuxedo instead of slacks and a white shirt for our wedding."

He sighed. "That's a nice thought but you know I'm not wearing no tux, baby, so stop asking me. I ain't trying to look all uptight on the day I take you to be my wife. That ain't my thing. I only own three suits anyway and they're all for when I'm out with my mother." He kissed me on my shoulder. "But what else were you thinking about? Because I know it was something good."

I giggled knowing where this was going. "That's it and that's all, Luke." I turned around to face him and my eyes rolled over his tatted up bare chest. "Why, what did you think I was thinking about?"

"I know what I want you to think about."

I sighed. "Luke, we aren't having sex until we get married."

"But why?" he kissed my lips and pulled away. "Don't you miss me being inside of you?"

Of course I did but I couldn't let him know my reasons. I was getting my HIV test back today and I would never dream of infecting him due to a situation that didn't involve him. So I had to wait and I was going to do whatever I had to do to keep him safe.

"You know I miss you inside of me but I want this to be right, Luke. We have the rest of our lives together to have sex. Just give me these next few weeks...okay?"

SHAY HUNTER

He looked over at me. "You got it but can I ask you something else?"

"Anything."

"Are you still angry about what happened at the church? If you are I really want to talk about it so we can clear the air right now."

I sat up and leaned against the headboard. He did the same thing. "First let me be clear, me not having sex with you has nothing to do with that. And yes, I am hurt but I know you love me."

"Do you also know that I wouldn't do anything to hurt you on purpose? I mean can you tell that from the moment I met you, you were and are the only woman for me?"

"That's just it. I'm not a woman, Luke. The chick you were with on the steps of the church *is* a woman. I'm a…I'm a…" my voice trailed off and my head lowered.

"You are my woman," he said as he pushed my chin up softly so that our eyes met. "You're mine. And just so you know, the only reason I was with her in the first place was for my mother. I was trying to make her happy."

I frowned in confusion. "But what about me being happy?"

"I would die for your happiness, Charlie."

"That's what you say but your actions are different. I mean do you know how it felt when I saw you with her? Even if I explained it to you, words wouldn't suffice. I was devastated, Luke, and I started questioning our entire life together."

"Baby, I wish you had brought this up back then."

"What are you talking about?"

"When I talked to you about my mother and her position at church. I knew you didn't want to talk about what happened on the steps of that church when you first moved in but we're going to talk about it now. My mother wanted me to take that chick to church so that she would be in a better position to get the job she always dreamed of. She figured that if they knew her son was gay they wouldn't give it to her. Rumors had been circulating about my sexuality and she was worried that they would pass her over."

"You could've told me."

"What are you talking about?" he stood up and slipped his plum colored silk robe on before walking to my side of the bed. He sat down. "I did tell you. You don't remember when we were at Flemings? The day that woman came and asked about her son?"

SHAY HUNTER

I did remember the day but I didn't remember him telling me he was taking no bitch to church. "You didn't tell me that you were taking her. We would've definitely had a sit down."

"I did, baby. I told you. At some point you zoned out and I got upset. Play the tapes back in your mind. I would've never done no shit like that without letting you know first. Are you fucking crazy? I love you, Charlie!"

When I looked into his eyes I knew he was dead serious. That night he took me out to dinner I was thinking about Belize walking into my bedroom and seeing Dixie. He was telling me about his mother's situation at the church but I didn't care because I was on some other shit at the time. He even got upset because I wasn't paying him any attention. All this time we broke up and it was my fault not his.

"I'm so sorry, baby," I said as a tear rolled down my face. "I violated our relationship when you didn't do anything but be honest with me."

"You didn't violate our relationship," he said wiping my face. "I just needed to make myself clearer. This is my fault not yours."

But it was my fault. Had I known he told me at the restaurant I would've never fucked dude in the bathroom.

There was a knock at the door and he walked toward the living room to answer it. I eased on my pink robe and followed him. When the door opened I saw his mother, Rose, on the other side. He lowered his head, looked back at me and allowed her inside.

"Hi, son," she said softly. She looked at me. "Hello, Charlie."

I smiled. That's all I could do because I wasn't sure if I liked her anymore.

"Luke, what happened to you yesterday? You were supposed to be coming to church with me."

He wiped his hand down the side of his face and sat down at the kitchen table. "Ma, I can't do that for you anymore. I'm so sorry. I really wanted to be there for you because I knew you needed me, and you have never been anything but supportive of me. But I almost lost my relationship behind that situation and it can't happen again. I hope you understand, ma. I really do."

She exhaled and touched her son's face. "I do understand, baby, and I'm sorry if I put you in an uncomfortable position. That was not my intention." She kissed him on the top of the head and walked toward me.

"Charlie, I'm so sorry. In my journey to the position I wanted I never stopped to think about what it would do to my son or to you. But you need to know something and I want this to be clear, I love you for my son. I told him that many times before and he can vouch for me."

I smiled at Luke. I knew he was perfect but this just made things better.

"When I look into your eyes I can tell you love him, and although I never imagined this life for my baby, I did imagine him happy and I can tell that he has that with you." She kissed me on my cheek. "I'm also going to say this. I don't know how y'all are going to do it but you will give me some grandbabies if it's the last thing you do."

I giggled.

"Ma, please don't start," Luke chuckled.

She looked back at him. "I'm dead serious," she said turning toward me.

"Thank you, ma'am," I said. "Your support means the world to me."

"Then you have it. And although you don't need them, I wanted you to know that you have my blessings too."

She kissed me on the cheek again and walked out. It was only fitting that the perfect man had the perfect mother.

SHAY HUNTER

CHAPTER EIGHTEEN

Charlie

I was doing Ryan's—the girl Monday gave my number to—butt injections in a motel in Virginia. She ended up being a really nice person and when I heard she was about to give away her son's college fund just to get the procedure I decided to do the injections. I knew if she went shopping around for another person they would've taken advantage of her generosity and I didn't want that.

Although I was working, my mind was on two things at the moment. First I was getting my HIV results back today and secondly her pussy stank so badly it caused my eyes to water.

I never understood why some females who came to get injections insisted on not washing. You are lying in a motel room with no panties on and your ass in the air. I mean really, be considerate.

Through everything that I had endured she smelled so bad that even if she did wash I wasn't sure that it would eliminate the problem. It smelled more like she had an infection than anything else.

"Thank you so much, Charlie," she said as her face scrunched up in pain as I inserted my needle. "I was afraid I would have to go somewhere else. And some of them chicks who have injections be looking lopsided out here."

"You're welcome," I paused to insert some more silicone into the needle. "Ryan, why do you feel like you have to do this so badly? I mean, I know what you told me about working at the strip club but you have a nice body already."

She giggled. "I'm surprised you are even asking me why I want injections. You're supposed to want clients to come to you so that you can get that money."

"Baby, I have enough paper to be setup for awhile. I'm doing this work just to pass the time."

"I get it," she smiled as sweat poured down her face.

SHAY HUNTER

I guess the discomfort of having silicone pressed into her body was getting to her. You had to be a G to handle the pain for the first time so I was surprised at how well she was doing.

"I really am doing it because I want to stand out at the strip club and my father suggested them. He always knows what's best."

"Your father?"

"Yeah, he's my manager. He sets up all of my appointments and manages my money. I don't even get to keep the cash because he puts it up in a bank account for me. He'll tell me every now and again how much money I saved but it doesn't matter because I trust him."

Wow. I knew what was going on even if this little girl didn't. So after I finished the last injection and placed the Krazy Glue and cotton on the site I sat on the edge of the bed and subjected myself to a few more minutes of the smell from her body.

"Ryan, you need to take better care of your body."

"What you mean?" she asked sliding into her sweat pants.

"Baby, I could smell your vagina the moment you walked into the room. That's not cool. You're too pretty for that."

"You can really smell me?" she asked with her jaw hung. "I'm so embarrassed."

"Yes, honey. You didn't know?"

She shook her head no.

I sighed. "Didn't your mother teach you how to care for yourself?"

"No," she said lowering her head. "She died when I was fifteen years old, but before that, she was too sick to ever teach me anything."

I knew her father was some shit. Any man who would let his daughter strip and be her manager had to be foul. Suddenly I wanted to be somewhat of a mentor to her.

"Look, I have to go but I want you to call me. I don't know a lot about life but I'm finding some things out along the way and I would love to help you. That is if you need it."

"Yes I need it," she said as her face lit up. "Thank you, Ms. Charlie. You have officially made my day and I can tell that we will be the best of friends."

SHAY HUNTER

I was in my old house grabbing a few things. Both Luke and Belize told me to wait but I was certain that Dixie was gone far away. After all, if he wasn't he would've done something to me by now. I thought maybe hitting me over the head with the bat was the last thing he planned to do to me and I was starting not to be as scared.

I had almost grabbed everything I wanted when I found a box full of pictures under my bed of me and Dixie before the bad times. I laughed at a few of them and a single tear ran down my face when I saw one of me and Dixie in this house. He was my best friend and I couldn't believe after all of this time we had come to this. We used to be in each other's corners and now we were sworn enemies.

I was collecting the rest of my things when I heard some activity in the front room. I grabbed my God Gun from my purse and approached the area cautiously. If it was Dixie, he was about to be finished once and for all because I had all intentions on shooting to kill. But I was shocked when I bent the corner and saw that it was Emma standing in my living room instead.

CHAPTER NINETEEN

Charlie

"You know I always had an idea that my son was gay," Emma said as we sat at the bar and nursed our third round of drinks. She tended to a Corona and I was drinking straight vodka, no ice. "But I tried to tell myself that it was all in my mind, you know? As if it would be better for both of us that way. But when I saw it with my own eyes, I knew the nature of our relationship would change forever."

"What happened?" Thinking about how rude I was being by asking, probably due to the drinks, I felt terrible. "I'm sorry, Emma. Forgive my rudeness. You don't have to answer if you don't want to."

She waved her hand. "Don't you worry about it, doll. As many times as I busted into your house unwanted, I'd consider your question warranted."

We both laughed before it simmered down, as if someone lowered the volume on the humor.

She took a large gulp of her beer and stared at the bottles of liquor on the wall. "I was supposed to be working from 9:00 a.m. until 10:00 p.m. that day. It was one of those four-day work-week things I used to do when I was a security guard for the hospital. But for some reason that day I didn't feel like working. I wasn't sick or anything like that; I just didn't feel like staying.

"Now that I look back I believe it had something to do with my intuition. Because in my heart I knew something was different with Fergie and I guess I wanted to go home and be there with him."

"Had you two fought earlier?"

"No, doll. We hardly ever fought," she grinned. "We were truly close, except for this one thing." She took another sip. "Well after an hour I was finally able to get someone to cover my shift. I could've called him and told him I was on my way home but I didn't. So when I walked into the living room they were right there, him and Rich, his best friend."

I saw tears roll down her face but she seemed unbothered by them, like she cried so much that it was a regular emotion as normal as laughing.

"Rich had Fergie bent over the edge of the couch while he was having sex with him, I guess in his rectum." She shook her head.

I gasped. I don't know if it was because I was drinking or the fact that she said rectum. I'd never heard boy on boy sex being described in such a technical way.

"I went off on him, Charlie." She looked into my eyes. "I took to scratching the brown skin off of Fergie's back and even cracked a lamp over Rich's head. To this day Rich is wearing the scar I gave him even though he's long since forgiven me.

"I didn't talk to Fergie for a week after that and it wasn't because he didn't try. The poor thing begged me almost every night to say one word to him, and took to sleeping on the floor at the bottom of my bed in the hopes that I would at least say excuse me before stepping over him."

She exhaled. "It took a week for me to come around and that's only because I found out he stopped going to school. We never talked about that day and I preferred it that way. The most trag-

SHAY HUNTER

ic part is I never forgave myself for how I be-
haved. He needed my support, not my condemna-
tion."

I rubbed her shoulder. "Aw, Emma, I remember Fergie and if there is one thing I know
it's that he loves his mother. Don't come down so
hard on yourself. Most parents react similarly.
You came around and that's all that matters."

She exhaled. "You are such a sweet child.
Tell me about your mother."

The moment she said that my heart beat rapidly. "My mother died when I was young and my
father was left to care for me. He hated me
though. Could never come around and accept me
for who I was: a gay teenager. So when I was in
high school he put me out after I came home with
a beaten face, courtesy of someone I had given my
body to."

"Why would he hurt you? If you were the
one injured?"

"He didn't want anybody knowing how I ob-
tained my bruises I guess." I shrugged. "The sad-
dest part is I never told anybody that I had sex
with my abuser. It got out when someone I cared
about guessed and told him. He beat me up at a

party. I guess my father used it as an excuse to abandon me and I haven't heard from him since."

"I feel so bad for you," she said with her eyes full of compassion. "You gotta know that it's hard for black men to deal with this type of thing. They haven't been given the tools necessary to talk with their children. I'm not making an excuse for him but I know he cared about you and just wasn't able to show you." She paused. "But what's going on with your life now? Who is that fine man I saw you with at the restaurant when we first reconnected?"

"Luke," I smiled. "He's my fiancé."

She clapped. "Oh my goodness, you two are going to look so great together. Straight out of a magazine! My stars!"

She was overly excited for me and that caused my stomach to jump. Despite her busting into my house today unannounced yet again, I had some good things going on. First I found out that I was HIV negative and I realized Emma wasn't out to ruin my world. She just wanted to find her son.

"You are so sweet, thank you," I said blushing. "I do love him and I'm sure he loves me too."

"I'm serious. You seem to be such a nice young lady, and even if your father doesn't know it, he would be blessed to have you in his life."

Her love and consideration caused my heart to tremble and I cried long and hard as she held me in her arms. I realized we probably looked foolish at the bar but I needed her warmth. I needed the compassion from an older mother figure and she was more than willing to give it to me, and I decided to give her a gift.

I separated from her, wiped my eyes and said, "I'm going to take you to Fergie."

Her jaw dropped and she closed her mouth in preparation to make her next statement. She swallowed and took a deep breath. "Will he be alive?"

"No. But he is resting in peace."

Tranny 911: *Dixie's Rise*

CHAPTER TWENTY

Charlie

I leaned back in the passenger seat of Belize's car, feeling sick to my stomach. It was a hangover. I overdid it last night when I had drinks with Emma but time and my senses got away from me. Luke was angry when I came home drunk out of my mind, and he even hinted at me possibly cheating on some get back shit, because of the church event.

Since I was HIV negative I dropped to my knees and showed him how much he meant to me and I didn't have any more problems from him. He went to sleep with a smile on his face and me in his arms.

But my problems didn't stop or end there. Now Emma knew that I was aware that her son was not alive. She sucked it up and handled it like a G when I told her he was buried but I didn't know if that was all a façade. Would she have the police waiting on me when I took her to her son's grave? Or would she kill me since I didn't tell her that I wasn't responsible for his death, just that I knew he was dead?

What was wrong with me? This was all so stupid and I didn't want to do anything but crawl up under Luke's big arms and go to sleep. But Belize was relentless. She even went as far as getting me dressed for wherever she wanted to take me and I knew the only way I could get rid of her was if I went with her.

"What's on your mind, Charlie?" Belize asked as she continued down the highway. "I haven't heard you this quiet since you got back with Luke."

"Nothing is on my mind," I said quickly. There was no way on Planet Earth that I would tell her that I killed someone, buried two bodies or told Emma. I would never hear the last of it.

"Wow, you said pretty quick."

"What I'm going through is private and there is nothing that can be done about it. I'm just thinking, Belize. I don't have to tell you every single thing that is going on in my mind, you know? So let's leave it at that."

She left me to it and when she finally stopped driving we were in the parking lot of Club Wiggles…in the daytime. "What are we doing here?" Although it wasn't during regular hours, the parking lot was kind of full.

"Just like it's none of my business about what's going on in your mind, it's none of your business about what's going on here." She parked her car. "Now get your stuff and come on."

I didn't feel like this shit today but whatever. I grabbed my purse and reluctantly followed her into the club. The moment she pushed the doors open I felt like I was transported to a whimsical world. First of all it looked nothing like the place known for its transvestites, tricks and closeted queens. It resembled an enchanting palace, something straight out of a children's story.

All my friends were standing in front of me with colorful gowns and they looked gorgeous. A large pearl colored banner that read "Congratulations, Oh Beautiful One" spanned from one side of the club to the other.

All I could do was cry before I walked inside and trannies with extra big hair, hard chests and muscular arms bombarded me with hugs. As crazy as it may have appeared to the outside world, these creative beasts were truly my family.

Belize grabbed my hand softly and walked me further inside as I marveled at all of the decorations. I could feel that a lot of love had gone into making this special for me.

"So this is why you dragged me from up under my man?" I asked Belize, trying to make jokes instead of more tears.

"Yes, and it was hard as hell too," she giggled. "Do you like it? We all pitched in to make it nice."

I twirled around with my arms out beside me. "I love it!"

Belize stopped my spin by placing both hands on my shoulders and said, "Great, because we aren't done yet."

She pulled me over to a table dressed with a white silk tablecloth. On top of it were about fifteen gifts covered in beautiful, sparkly wrapping paper. I was placed down in a seat that resembled a silver throne and I was overwhelmed with joy.

"Is all of this for me?" I asked Belize, already knowing the answer.

"Well it damn sure ain't for this monkey face bitch," Kenya interjected looking at Goldie.

"Or your dried up, stank hole, no having a—"

"Girls," Belize screamed at Kenya and Goldie. "Unfortunately this isn't about either of you wilder beasts. So either jump back into the wild or let my baby have her moment." She looked down at me and handed me a small gold-wrapped box. "The first one is from me." She placed her hand on her chest. "I pray you love it."

I smiled as I ripped and scratched the paper as if it did me wrong. When I finally got into the center I was looking at a black leather box. I opened it carefully and my eyes lit up as I stared at a picture of me and Luke inside of a gold locket. It was taken when he was over my house during a Spades party. We had both just kicked ass and we were cuddled up grinning.

Belize had been snapping pics all night and I remembered being irritated. Of course now I felt like an idiot because she used her skills for good. Normally she would hoard the pics and not let anyone see them. This time was different.

I gripped her tightly and said, "Thank you so much, B. Thank you for being the friend I never knew I deserved."

I saw her eyes watering but she stopped them by wiping the tears roughly away, smearing her mascara in the process. "Don't worry about all that. Open the rest of your gifts."

I went through gift after gift and was in awe at the thought and consideration placed into everything. I had necklaces, sexy negligees, gift cards and more. I expressed gratitude to everyone who was present and even those who couldn't be there but who still bought me a gift.

My last present was a huge red box with a gold bow on top. "Who is this from?"

I looked around the room and waited for an answer. All of the queens shrugged and most of them had already shown me what they'd gotten me. So what was this?

"Read the card first, honey," Belize suggested.

"You're right." I removed the small red card from the top with a smile on my face.

"Read it out loud," Kenya suggested, standing behind me.

I looked up at her and grinned. "Okay, okay, don't lose your breasts," I joked, trying to appease the crowd. I cleared my throat and eyed the card. "Dear Charlie, I lost my beauty long ago and now it's time to destroy yours."

By the time I realized what I actually read everyone was gasping. With my mind now clear, I popped the box open. Inside was a picture of me with a disfigured face. It looked like it was Photo shopped.

I dropped the picture and screamed.

SHAY HUNTER

CHAPTER TWENTY-ONE

Charlie

I sat on the sofa next to Luke at his house as he rubbed my arm. Belize sat across from us looking like a distraught mother.

"Baby, it's going to be alright," Luke said to me. "Dude is just mad because you happy and he's a miserable faggy. Don't let him get to you."

Luke was consoling me but I knew my man. I could see the muscles in his arms tightening and I could feel the strength in his grip as he held me. You see Luke was a fighter to his core. As a matter of fact, the first time I ever laid eyes on him he was in jail for a scuffle. He was in a cell with blood covering his body and clothes. Seeing me like this probably brought up violent memories and I'm sure he wanted to get even.

"I can't believe Dixie would do this shit to me," I yelled remembering how she destroyed my bridal shower. "Why won't she leave me alone? I don't understand!"

By the time I had asked that question Belize had cleared her throat three times even though I ignored her. She was trying to get my attention and I knew what she was trying to hint at without words. She wanted me to tell Luke what was really going on because I kept my real ordeal away from him.

"Honey, maybe you should tell him everything," Belize suggested looking into my eyes. "He has a right to know because you don't want this fool walking up on him without him being prepared."

Belize said so much that she might as well have told him the rest. But as much as I hated to admit it she was right. Luke had no idea the type of beef I had in these streets with Dixie. In his mind I was a sweet nurse who led a drama free life. Boy was he wrong.

"What's up, bae?" he asked positioning his body to look into my eyes. "What is she talking about?"

SHAY HUNTER

Before I said anything to him I turned around to look at Belize. Then I threw up both fuck you fingers to express my opinion of her at the moment. Belize wore a smile and was untethered by my attitude.

I went on to explain to Luke the version of facts I'd given to everybody up to this point. That version, my favorite of course, left out the part where anybody died or was murdered. Instead I explained that Dixie was dangerous and I had to do what I could to prevent him from killing somebody by way of paralyzing him. Luke's face alternated between anger and worry and when I was done with everything his expression rested on concern.

"Why wouldn't you tell me this, bae? I can't believe you kept this dude in your house all this time and I didn't know. And then he hits you over the head with a bat? What if he would've killed you?"

"I didn't want you to leave me, Luke. It was embarrassing keeping him like that but I really thought he would hurt somebody."

"Leave you?" he chuckled. "Are you serious? You don't get it, do you? I'm not going anywhere, Charlie. If anything you should've told me what was going on so that I could have had your back in that shit." He stood up. "Let me make a few phone calls. I'll be right back."

Luke was on the phone in his kitchen for ten minutes. When he returned he said, "Okay, I have some people who will be watching your back over the next few days, until I can have all of your things moved into my house."

"Luke, I don't need no—"

"Don't tell me what you don't need," he said aggressively. "You obviously need a lot and I'm not going to leave you alone to get hurt again. And if you love me you wouldn't ask me that shit."

"He's right, Charlie," Belize said. "You should let him—"

"Please go home, B," I yelled. "You've done enough over here in my household."

She grabbed the collar of her dress. "Well I never." She stood up, yanked her purse and switched out of the front door.

When she was gone Luke said, "She cares about you, Charlie. She's different from the others and you should keep her around."

"I may consider it on one condition."

"There you go with your conditions."

"I'm serious. I want you to wear the tux for our wedding, baby. For me."

"Why do we have to keep going through this? I'm not interested in wearing no tux. Especially the one they delivered today with all of that extra bullshit that comes with it."

"But it would be for me. I'm begging you."

"Charlie, it's like this, if you want me to marry you in a tux then you obviously don't want the real me. So what do you want to do? Marry a fake?"

"I want you to be my husband so I guess I don't have a choice." When my cell phone rang with a blocked number I reluctantly answered.

"Charlie, it's Emma. I've been calling you all day. When are you going to take me to the place we talked about at the bar?"

I stood up and looked down at Luke. I didn't want him hearing my conversation. "I'll be right back, baby."

He frowned. "So you have to leave to talk on the phone now?"

"It's not about that," I said. "I just need to give privacy to my friend who doesn't want you knowing her business."

He raised his hands and dropped them in his lap before turning on the TV with the remote. "Do what you gotta do."

I walked to the kitchen. "Emma, I can't show you right now," I whispered. "I'm sorry."

"You better make time, Charlie. I like you but I need to know where my son is and I waited long enough. Now you said you know his whereabouts and I want to know them now!"

CHAPTER TWENTY-TWO

Charlie

I drove down the highway on the way to Strawberry Fields with Emma in the passenger seat of my car. If there was one thing that could be said about Emma it was that she was persistent. And since I got drunk and dumb at the bar and told her about Fergie, I had to see things through with her, even though I wasn't sure if I could trust her.

"Can I ask you something?" Emma asked digging into her purse. "It's kind of private."

"Sure," I shrugged. "What is it?"

She retrieved a pack of gum and leaned it toward me. I shook my head indicating I didn't want one. "When did you know that you were interested in men?"

I looked over at her. "Why, Miss Emma, if I wasn't sure I would say that the gay life fascinates you. Am I correct?"

I could see her blushing and she tried to get it together by looking out of her window. "It's not that. What fascinates me is the unordinary."

"And you think being gay is uncommon?"

"Not anymore, I guess. But at one point it was. If it were not true nobody would have a problem with it. Shit, I would go further and say in about fifty years nobody is going to care at all. But it always amazes me in this day and age when young men like yourself jump out there and do what your heart tells you even though it could backfire on you."

"I guess....for me anyway...I don't have a choice."

"Explain."

I sighed. "I'm not attracted to women at all, Emma. Just the idea of being with one makes me feel sick...that food poisoning kind of sick you know? I need a man to hold me and to make me feel safe. If I had to offer the same thing to a woman we would have a serious problem. Don't get me wrong, I respect the lesbians but it ain't for me."

She giggled. "I think I'm getting it." She paused. "So are you saying if you can't be with a man you can't survive?"

"That's exactly what I'm saying."

"I used to feel that way about one man in particular." She gazed out her window again. "It was Fergie's father and I think that's one of the reasons I couldn't deal with my son being gay at first. He looks so much like him that it's crazy."

I laughed.

"What's funny?" she asked.

"Nothing really. It's just that I always saw Fergie in drag and to me he resembled Dionne Warwick. So now I'm having to imagine Dionne Warwick as his father."

She laughed harder. "Well even Dionne had a father right?"

I shrugged. "You're right."

The car was silent for a moment.

"Charlie, when are you going to tell me what happened with my son. If he's buried and you are able to take me to him, it's obvious that you know more. Understand that the only reason I'm not scratching your eyes out right now is because I know your heart. And from being around you I am positive that you aren't capable of something like

Tranny 911: *Dixie's Rise*

this. So what happened to my boy? Just tell me now so I can have closure."

I told Emma about the injections procedure and how everything went down. I told her how Dixie allowed Fergie to die and how angry I was with him. As the story continued I saw Emma's expression grow darker and darker.

"That Dixie is a monster isn't he?" she asked.

I nodded yes.

"What did he do to you?" she continued. "To make you so angry?"

"I think the situation with Fergie is what sent me over the edge. Fergie didn't have to die, you know? He was still alive and had we called 911 he would be with you to this day. I hate Dixie the most because of that."

She shook her head. "I'm so angry right now but as long as I can bury my son, I'm going to put it away. I'm going to leave Dixie alone but it's not because I'm letting him have the upper hand. I've prayed long and hard and I need peace. I don't want to be angry or violent anymore because it has damaged my soul."

"What about me? Are you going to leave me alone too?"

"Well I had hoped that you would think of me as a friend instead of a bother."

I smiled. "You know what, Emma," I paused, "the strange thing is that I do consider you to be a friend." She placed her hand on my leg and smiled.

When we made it to Strawberry Fields I parked and we both got out of the car. The moment we climbed the hill I saw two piles of dirt in the place Fergie and Gi-Gi's bodies were buried. I knew immediately that something was up.

"Something is wrong," I said running toward the place where Fergie was buried. Emma followed behind me. "Something is really wrong."

"What is it?" Emma asked frantically.

I approached the hole and knew immediately what happened. Dixie had beaten us to the punch. She unearthed both bodies. "He's not here," I yelled looking into the brown hole that was once Fergie's home. "His body is not here."

Emma threw herself into the hole as if she was about to save him. While she was inside my phone rang and confused at what was going on, I answered. "Hello."

"Charlie, it's Belize! You have to come to my house now! It's an emergency!"

Tranny 911: Dixie's Rise

CHAPTER TWENTY-THREE

Charlie

I sped down the highway thinking about how weird this evening was turning out to be I finally decided to take Emma to see her son's grave only to discover that Dixie removed his body. What I wanted to know was where he'd taken them. Both of them.

Then there was Belize. She called me like her butthole was closed up and she was no longer able to use it. I wondered what she had to tell me that was so important. I tried to call her back to get more information when I dropped Emma off at her house but she was avoiding my call. I knew it had something to do with Dixie and my only question was what had he done now.

When my cell phone rang I hit the button in the car so that the speaker could come on. "Belize, is that you?"

SHAY HUNTER

"No, it's me. Ryan."

I sighed and rolled my eyes. "Ryan now is not a good time to talk."

"Why is it that you told me I could call you but whenever I do you, you avoid me? Was the friendship you extended to me all a lie?"

This chick was needy and I was starting to believe that I'd made a huge mistake by offering my friendship. "Ryan, right now I don't have time for this but I wish I did. Something is going on in my life and I have to tend to it. Now if you are tired of calling me you can wait for me to return your call instead, okay?"

The phone was silent and I had to look down at my handset to see if she was still on the line. "Hello," I said.

"I called you twenty times, and each time you ignored me. Remember this day."

She hung up and I was relieved. The chick had proven to be psychotic and unfortunately for her I didn't have any more room in my life for crazies. I was booked up with Dixie.

When I made it to Belize's house I didn't see her truck anywhere. So I parked and walked around to the back of her place to see if the light was on in her room. The entire house was pitch black and I knew she couldn't be inside.

I walked back to the car, got inside and called her five more times. She wasn't answering and I was starting to worry. I was about to call her again and contact the police when she pulled up and parked in her driveway. I hopped out of the car and waited for her to get out.

Belize slid out of the truck in a pair of tight jeans and a black jacket with my wedding gown over her arm covered in plastic. "Hey, honey. I didn't realize you were going to beat me here. How are you?"

"Hey, honey?" I repeated angrily. "Hey, honey! Do you realize I have been an emotional wreck waiting on you? What the fuck is wrong with you?"

Belize walked to the front door and I was on her heels. "What I want to know is what's wrong with you?" She walked inside and turned on the lights, placing my gown on the recliner. "You look like you want to kill me."

"Bitch, you called me and said to come over your house because it was an emergency. And when I get here you're not home. You know Dixie's crazy ass is roaming around and I thought something happened to you. You can't do people like that."

Belize laughed and that angered me because from my perspective wasn't shit funny. "Let me tell you something, Dixie is many things, but she's not crazy enough to come in my house. I would murder her first. Plus my dude be here all the time. And his tall ass don't give nobody a chance to do anything to me because he never leaves. I'm surprised he's not here now."

"B, you have to be careful these days," I tried to stress. "Dixie is out to ruin me and I have a feeling that he wants to destroy everything around me, including you."

She walked over toward me. "Look at you, so concerned about my well being and stuff." She hugged me and released me. "Don't you worry about none of that though. I'm going to be fine. Always have and always will."

I was done talking to her because it was obvious I was frustrated for nothing. I threw myself on the sofa and asked, "What was the emergency, B?"

"The emergency is that fucking clerk at Bells & Whistles. Do you know that after everything I needed done, that she still fucked up? I ended up having to get her manger involved. I was calling you all frantic because I thought we were going to have to try on another dress that a friend of mine made instead. And I wanted you here so that we could have it fitted in time for the wedding."

"Are you telling me that the emergency was the dress?"

"Yes."

I looked up at her and busted out in tears. I realized at that moment that I could no longer hide anything from her. I told her about Fergie and how she died. I told her that I helped bury the body and that I took Emma to see him only for him to be unearthed. In the end Belize looked frozen with fear.

"Charlie, my dear, dear Charlie, things are far worse for you than I thought."

"I know." I shook my head. "But what can I do? I don't know what to do anymore."

"At this point you have to sit back and wait for Karma to arrive. But if we pray, and I mean really hard, maybe in the end you'll survive."

CHAPTER TWENTY-FOUR

Charlie

Fleming's restaurant's private room was a beautiful place to hold our rehearsal dinner. As I looked at all of my friends, who were dressed conservatively, seated around the table, I couldn't help but feel grateful that Belize was in my life and was able to take care of everything. I didn't have to lift a finger. Even Luke's friends came out and they looked handsome and appeared to be having a good time too. Considering all my girls were trannies that was really cool.

Dinner was great and everything went without a hitch...so far anyway. As hard as I tried, I couldn't pull myself out of the hole I was in after seeing the picture and Fergie's empty burial site.

"I'd like to make an announcement, everyone," Luke said standing up as he clinked a fork on the edge of his glass. When he had our attention he sat the glass and fork down. "I want to thank everybody for sharing this special moment with me and my future wife." He placed his hand on my shoulder. "When I was younger I never thought I would find someone who I wanted to spend the rest of my life with. It was never even a thought of mine. But here I am, standing in front of you all and saying that I have met that special someone. I don't want to live my life without her and I made a decision that I'm not going to."

"I'm about to cry," Belize said covering her mouth with both hands.

He chuckled a little. "Hold off on that, B," he said jokingly. He looked down at me again. "I just want to say you mean the world to me, Charlie. And I'm going to spend the rest of my life showing you that."

Everyone clapped and he sat down. "It's your turn, baby," he said with a huge smile on his face.

I stood up and looked up and down the table at everyone. I wanted to say something profound but I had too much drama going on in my life to think of anything worthwhile.

SHAY HUNTER

The moment I opened my mouth I swallowed my words and ran away from the table. I ended up in a small sitting room across from the private area. I threw myself on the sofa and a second later Luke came in and closed the door behind him.

"Baby, what's wrong? Are you feeling okay?" he sat down next to me and rubbed my leg.

"Luke, I'm…I'm just…"

"You not thinking about backing out on me, are you?" he asked in a concerned tone. "Because I can't take that, baby. I'm letting you know that right now. I need you to come down that aisle and be my wife."

I wanted to let him know about Fergie's body being moved and that I was still worried that Dixie was somewhere waiting to ruin my entire life. But what if he got tired of it all and left me?

"I'm not having second thoughts. I'm just happy that's all. I swear to you."

He exhaled as if relieved. "If you're happy then why are you looking stressed out?"

"Because I'm about to get married to you tomorrow, Luke. It's a happy moment in my life and I don't want it to end. It's always been a dream and now it has finally come true. I can't wait to be your wife."

"I hope that's true." He kissed me on the cheek. "Because the way you ran out on our friends had me worried."

I shook my head realizing how ridiculous I must've looked. "What were they saying?"

"I told them you were probably nervous so they left it alone. Everyone cares about you so it's cool. And it's okay for you to have feelings, Charlie. Because you're right, it is a big step."

"I'll be okay but can you do something for me?"

"Something like what?"

"Wear the tuxedo I have for you. I'm begging you."

He turned away from me. "Baby, I told you I don't—"

"Luke, please wear the tux. Can't you see how much it means to me? Now more than ever?"

He turned toward me again. "Well if it will make you feel better I'll wear it."

"The entire thing?"

"Yes, baby," he said squeezing my chin lightly to pull my face toward him. "I'll wear everything. As always, you'll have your way."

CHAPTER TWENTY-FIVE

Charlie

Belize and me were in a large, beautiful suite in the *W Hotel* in Washington DC. I sat in front of a mirror while Belize pinned up my hair. This was the day I'd always dreamed of. The day my father and others told me would never happen for a boy like me and yet here I was, preparing to be a wife.

"What's on your mind, beautiful?" Belize asked as she placed a pearl tipped bobby pin in my bun. "You should be smiling instead of frowning. This is your wedding day."

"I'm not frowning."

She poked her lips out and placed her hands on her hips. "Charlie, you already know that I'm built for prying. So save yourself the trouble and time and tell me what's on your mind." She picked up the blinged out brush and continued working on my bun as I eyed my sad face in the mirror.

"It's nothing big. I just have the jitters."

She put the brush down and picked up her cell phone from the dresser. She scrolled through the pictures and stopped at one to show me. "Now are you sitting down there and telling me that you are confused about marrying this man? As fine as he is?"

I took the phone from her hand and my jaw dropped. "What are you doing with a picture of Luke in your phone?"

She picked up the brush again. "Shit, I got a picture of every nigga you ever fucked with." She brushed the side of my bun softly. "Well, at least the niggas I met of yours anyway." She looked at me before we both busted out in laughter.

I sat the phone down. "You are so crazy."

"I'm dead serious too." She looked at me. "Seriously, talk to me, honey. What's on your mind? I don't want you going down the aisle to meet your new husband with that face."

"I'm thinking about my mother and wondering how she would feel about me and Luke."

"Do you really want that thought to destroy your day? Because whether your mother accepts

SHAY HUNTER

you or not this day is not about her, Charlie. It's about you and your future husband."

I looked down at my pearl colored finger-nails that were sitting in my lap. "I wish that was enough."

Belize exhaled, sat the brush down and said, "Turn around."

"What do you mean?" I asked looking at her reflection in the mirror. "We have to be at the church in under an hour. Finish up my hair."

"I said turn around, Charlie. I'm serious. Anyway, it's considered fashionable for the bride to be a little late."

I turned around.

She took a deep breath and said, "Okay, so pretend that I am your mother and tell me what you want me to know?"

I tilted my head and giggled hard. "Belize, you taking this Mommy Dearest shit too far now. I mean really." I shook my head. "Finish my hair so we can leave; I'm getting mad now."

"But I'm serious, Charlie. I'm not doing any-thing else until we work through this. Now talk to me. Tell me what you would want me to know as your mother."

When I peered into her eyes I could tell that something else was going on. This was unlike the other times. Belize really wanted me to have peace and this was one of the reasons I loved her so much.

"Okay...I'll play along." I sighed. I took a few more moments to compose myself. "Mama...today is the most important day of my life. I have met a man who loves me and cherishes me but I still feel unworthy. Part of the reason is that I know you would never approve, and the other part is that before him, I never knew true love existed." I exhaled again. "I guess what I'm trying to say is are you happy for me? Would you still love me even if I married a man?"

Belize smiled lightly and looked down at me. "Charlie, this is your life," she said with compassion heavy in her voice. "It always has been. Neither I nor your father had the right to make you feel that it was anything but. What I want to say to you now is that I'm proud of you. I'm proud of the woman that you've become despite the things that you have gone through. You are strong, Charlie, and no matter what, I want you to never forget that. You are truly the daughter I never knew I wanted and I love you very much."

SHAY HUNTER

Belize held me in her arms and I cried for about a minute. It was just what I needed and even though it was an act, oddly enough I felt empowered.

When I was done and looked up at Belize, she was crying too. "Look at what you did to your mascara," she said reaching for a makeup sponge to fix my face. "Don't you know that brides don't cry?"

I grabbed her hand softly and said, "Thank you, Belize."

"It's nothing," she said sniffling a little. "Besides, what's a queen to do?"

I was in the white limousine, about two minutes from the church and something in my heart told me that something was off. I looked over at Belize who was on the phone finalizing the last few pieces for the ceremony.

When she was done she stuck her phone in her purse and said, "What's wrong? You look scared."

"Can you feel it?" I asked her placing my hand over my heart.

"Feel what?"

"Something is off, Belize. Way off."

She sighed heavily, like I was getting on her last nerves. "What are you talking about now?" she asked fanning me off. "I done re-enacted your mama, took care of all the details for the reception and made sure everybody was on time. It's time to stop making excuses and start living the rest of your life."

We pulled up in front of the church and it felt like the breath was pulled from my body.

Looking out of the window, I couldn't believe the sight. Slowly my head rotated toward her and I asked, "You still going to tell me that I'm wrong?"

SHAY HUNTER

CHAPTER TWENTY-SIX

Charlie

I slowly crawled out of the limousine with a heavy heart. I looked up at the large white church with the huge gold cross sitting on top of it. Instead of it bringing me peace and serenity, I was overcome with fear. There was absolutely nobody standing in the front. Where was everyone?

Belize walked behind me, grabbing at the train of my wedding dress as I quickly made my way up the steps.

When I arrived at the top I pulled open the double cherry wood doors. Inside I saw a house full of people sitting in their seats but they appeared slumped over as if they were asleep.

"What's going on, Belize?" I asked, my words accompanied by heavy breaths. "What's happening?"

"I don't know, baby," she said in a whisper. "But this is not good at all."

When I looked toward the front of the chapel I saw several men lying down. I picked up the train of my wedding dress and rushed toward the front, past all of the pews and people slumped over. When I looked back to see the front of their bodies as I made my way to the alter, I noticed everyone was covered in blood. Some people had bullet holes in their foreheads and others had them in their chests.

I heard Belize scream as I continued to the front and figured she was finally seeing the horror too. Everyone was murdered. I realized I wasn't breathing regularly and had to take quick breaths to prevent myself from passing out.

When I made it to the alter I scanned over the men who were supposed to be groomsmen. I even stepped over a few bodies trying to find my baby. I didn't want to be heartless but I was only interested in one man, my fiancé. So where was he?

When I finally found him I dropped to my knees and lifted up his head. His eyes were closed and the rest of my breath felt as if it had been suctioned out of my body.

SHAY HUNTER

"Oh my, God," I cried as I sat down and placed his head in my lap. I looked at a statue of Jesus hanging on a cross over my head. "Why would you do this to me, God? Why didn't you let me have him? Why?"

"Baby," I heard him whisper.

I wiped my tears and looked down at Luke's face. Was he actually talking? His eyes were open and he was staring up at me. Remembering his tuxedo, I tore at his jacket and shirt until I found what I was looking for...the bulletproof vest that was apart of the tuxedo I made him wear.

"You wore it," I sobbed while wiping my eyes. One of my lashes fell off and landed on his forehead. "You wore it. You wore the vest."

He smiled lightly considering the situation. "Yes, baby. I did. But the bullet still pierced my chest a little and I need help."

"Call the police," I yelled at Belize. "Luke is alive!"

I focused back on Luke. I was overwhelmed with relief even though I also felt guilty. As I looked around the church, there was nothing but death and carnage. And yet the man I loved more than anything had survived it all because he kept his promise.

Tranny 911: Dixie's Rise

"I'm getting you some help, baby. But who did this?"

"You know," he said as he winced a little in pain.

I shook my head no. "I don't. Who?"

"Dixie."

My body swayed a little. In the midst of everything that was happening I didn't stop to think that just a month or so earlier someone had vowed to take everything away from me. And had Luke not worn the bulletproof vest, he would've been successful.

When I heard the sirens in the background I figured Belize must have called the police and my fear was slightly diminished.

"I'm so sorry I got you into this, Luke. I—,"

"You didn't do anything but try and be happy. And even though I didn't get a chance to make you my wife today, I won't stop until that day comes."

I was in the hospital's lobby in a bloody wedding dress with Belize, Kenya and Goldie. We lost a lot of friends today, a lot of people we loved

SHAY HUNTER

and cared about who came to see my wedding and it was all for nothing. Despite the events, all three of them had taken the time to be with me to make sure Luke was okay.

I was sitting on a blue plastic seat, waiting on the doctor to tell me something. Belize sat next to me and put a soft hand on my knee. "I can't imagine what you're going through right now, Charlie. So I'm not going to make a statement that would insult you. I just want you to know that I'm here."

"I can't believe this," I said looking out ahead of me at others waiting on news about their loved ones. "I can't believe Dixie went so far." I looked over at Belize. "How could she?"

"Dixie is not well, Charlie. You knew that more than anybody and I should've listened to you. A person capable of this kind of evil is not human and you shouldn't put this on your heart."

"It's so hard. This was my wedding and a lot of people died because of me."

"And that's why you need to be strong. I don't want you feeling sorry for yourself anymore. I want you to be tough and do what you have to do to bring this nigga to justice. You spoke to the police today?"

"Yeah, but I didn't really tell them anything."

"Well maybe you should. They aren't going anywhere."

"Are you Charlie?" a doctor with piercing blue eyes asked stepping up to me.

I stood up and rubbed my arms. It was cold in the hospital and I didn't have anything on my shoulders. "I am."

"Luke is well and he's asking for you. Can you follow me?"

I quickly walked behind the doctor. He led me to an open doorway. "There he is. You have five minutes before we have to come back and run some more tests."

When he left I rushed over to the bed. The IV in his arm did not stop me from gripping him and pulling him into me. When I was done I sat on a chair next to the bed and held his hand.

"How do you feel?"

"I'm fine, baby," he chuckled. "I told you that. Stop worrying."

I kissed his hand. "This is so bad, Luke. Twenty-eight people were murdered today. I feel like it's all my fault."

SHAY HUNTER

"Why would you say something like that? I told you at the church that it wasn't your fault. It was that faggy nigga Dixie who did this and when I get out of this hospital I'm going to find him and show him how I feel about him."

I stared into his eyes. I saw the rage and I felt the anger in the way he gripped my hand. He'd lost a lot of friends today and yet he wanted to avenge my name. I couldn't let him do this because Belize was right. I needed to man up and take care of business myself. After all, I made my bed and I had to lie in it.

I kissed the top of his hand and released my hold. "I can't let you do that, Luke."

"Fuck you mean you can't let me do that?"

"Just what I said. This is my fault and I have to see to it that he doesn't hurt anybody again." I stood up and gripped the bottom of my dress. "I'm sorry, Luke, but it's over."

He tried to sit up in bed but the machines stuck to his body prevented him. "Fuck you mean it's over?"

"I'm letting you go."

"No, what you mean is you're leaving me," he yelled. "After everything I've been through, after everything I've lost already. Is that what you're telling me? As I lay in the hospital for a bullet I took for you, you're going to walk out on me?"

"I'm saying that I'm leaving you so that you won't have to suffer again." I walked backwards toward the door. "I really am sorry, Luke."

I ran away.

SHAY HUNTER

CHAPTER TWENTY-SEVEN

Charlie

I sat in Emma's kitchen, at her breakfast bar, nursing my second bottle of vodka. I was still wearing the bloody wedding dress I was supposed to get married in yesterday. Emma was standing in front of me, her body draped in a cotton baby blue robe and she had huge pink rollers in her grey hair.

"You have to be the strongest woman I know," Emma said pouring herself some vodka in a yellow coffee cup.

"Me?" I asked pointing to myself. "How do you figure?" I giggled at the thought alone.

"Look at everything you've been through and yet you still manage to move and survive. That's admirable."

Tranny 911: *Dixie's Rise*

I laughed. "You call this surviving? Can't you see the blood leaving my body, Emma? I'm almost dead."

She sat her cup down and raised the sleeves of her robe. She turned her arms up so that I could see the crease of her arm. I saw a bunch of raised knife wounds.

I ran my hand over one of them. It was thick and hard and it felt like a worm was under her skin. "What happened?"

"I tried to kill myself by slicing at my arteries." She pulled the sleeves down and picked up her coffee cup. "But as usual, I was unsuccessful because someone called the ambulance and I was rescued." She shook her head and laughed. "I can't do the slightest things right."

"What made you wanna...you know...take your own life?"

"Losing my boy. Once you're a parent I pray you never have to go through what I'm going through now. And to think that Dixie had something to do with it, it just boils my blood. I trusted him. I allowed him into my house and he took my son's life. No offense, but I should've choked the life out of him when I came to your house that day."

SHAY HUNTER

"No offense taken. He's a monster," I said honestly. I downed all of my vodka before pouring another cup. "And I don't know why it took me so long to notice. I was actually his friend and everybody tried to get me to see what I never could."

"It's not you, young Charlie. Some people choose to be blind. There is safety in not seeing what is in front of you. When you're blind you don't have to make the decisions necessary to live your own life." She exhaled. "I was like that before, with Fergie's father. There wasn't a thing I wouldn't do for him and it still wasn't enough. He wanted more."

"We've all played the fool."

"But not like me, Charlie," she poured herself another hefty coffee cup of vodka before refilling mine. "Fergie's father is in jail for child sexual abuse."

"What?"

"He was sexually abusing his own son for years and I turned my head on purpose. I wanted to…I wanted to ignore it because I wanted to keep my son and my husband when what I should have done was leave the marriage and murder him. I think that's why when I saw Fergie with his best friend it messed up my mind. To this day I don't know if my son was gay because he was born that way, or if his own father made him like that."

"I'm gay and I wasn't raped. I really believe I was born this way." Charlie said.

Emma cried heavily and I stood up and held her tightly. Somewhere along the line, in the midst of the pain and heartache, I found a real friend in Emma. She was like a mother figure and being around her comforted me. Perhaps it was the fact that she was the one person on earth who hated Dixie as much as I did. I can't really call it. All I know for sure is that we were connected.

"Let's be brave for once in our lives," Emma protested when we separated.

"How?" I wiped my wet face.

"Let's find this mothafucka and put him out of his misery."

"Who? Dixie?"

"Is there anyone else?"

"But how? I mean, where would he be?"

"You know the answers to that, Charlie."

"I don't." I shook my head. "I don't talk to him at all."

"I'm not talking about now. I'm talking about back then. Humans are creatures of habit and their habits don't change too often. Tonight we will drink and toast. And tomorrow you will remember every conversation, every person and every event he ever told you about and you will write it down. When you have a clear list we will compile the information, find him and take his life."

EPILOGUE

New York

6 MONTHS LATER

Dixie was leaning over the bar trying to flag the bartender, who was purposely ignoring him, down for the tenth time for another drink. His full beard, which concealed his botched up face, was soaked with Hennessy and yet he wanted another. Dressed like a man's man in a black sweater, jeans and boots, he decided that his time in New York would best be spent on the cute females lingering at the end of the bar.

Drunk out of his mind and with his breath smelling like a sock full of shit he pushed up on the beautiful woman on his right. "What you drinking? 'Cause I got it."

The woman turned around, took one look at him and inhaled his funky breath before getting up.

"Fuck you then, you flat face bitch," he yelled as he watched her walk away.

Frustrated Dixie, who now went by Dixon, placed his head on the bar and closed his eyes. Life for him had been anything but easy lately. First he had to get rid of Fergie and Gi-Gi's bodies by throwing them in the Anacostia River like he did Nurse Aggy. All because he was afraid that Charlie would lead Emma there, and he had. And then after he went into the wedding chapel and killed all those people with a machine gun, he was angry when he learned that the man he was gunning for had survived.

Dixie couldn't understand how it seemed that everything he tried to do to Charlie backfired. What was he, some kind of protected angel?

It was then that he made a decision that fucking with Charlie wasn't worth it anymore. Not only that, but he wasn't trying to answer to the homicide he left in his wake. So he decided to start all over, maybe find a wife who would take care of

him. Of course he would still be fucking men behind his wife's back but it didn't mean she would
have to know it.

Dixon was just about to go to sleep right
where he was when he felt a small hand on his
shoulder. He raised his head and was staring at
Charlie's beautiful face.

He blinked two times hoping to get her enchanting image out of his mind but she was still
there. "Hello, Dixie," Charlie said licking his
glossy lips. "How are you these days?"

Dixie's body shivered with fright. How did
he find him? "Uh…how did you know I was
here?"

"Aw, you forgot already?" he said slyly.
"Prior to you ruining my life, I knew everything
about you. We were the best of friends remember?
In fact you told me about this bar and how you
used to come down here and play butch every
now and again. You said when you had money the
bitches would be all over you." Charlie looked
around him. "Although I must say, you look aw-
fully lonely right now."

Remembering that he used to boss Charlie
around, Dixie stuck his chest out. "So what you
gonna do now? Try and fight me or something?"

SHAY HUNTER

"Of course not."

"That's right," he said cockily. "Because you know I would whip your fucking ass all up through this bar."

"I wouldn't dare try and fight you, Dixie," Charlie said placing his hair behind his ear. "I'm too pretty for that. Besides, we have a better plan."

"And what's—"

His sentence was halted when he felt a handgun press against his spine. When he looked over his shoulder he was staring in Emma's face. "Get up real smooth, Dixie. You coming with me."

Tranny 911: *Dixie's Rise*

SILENCE
OF THE
NINE

T. STYLES

NATIONAL BEST SELLING AUTHOR OF *RAUNCHY*

CARTEL PUBLICATIONS
PRESENTS

SHE WAS AN INMATE WIFE UNTIL
HE DID HER WRONG.

PRISON
THRONE

T. STYLES

NATIONAL BEST SELLING AUTHOR OF *RAUNCHY*

The Cartel Collection
Established in January 2008
We're growing stronger by the month!!!
www.thecartelpublications.com

Cartel Publications Order Form
Inmates <u>ONLY</u> get novels for $10.00 per book!

Titles	*Fee*
Shyt List	$15.00
Shyt List 2	$15.00
Pitbulls In A Skirt	$15.00
Pitbulls In A Skirt 2	$15.00
Pitbulls In A Skirt 3	$15.00
Pitbulls In A Skirt 4	$15.00
Victoria's Secret	$15.00
Poison	$15.00
Poison 2	$15.00
Hell Razor Honeys	$15.00
Hell Razor Honeys 2	$15.00
A Hustler's Son 2	$15.00
Black And Ugly As Ever	$15.00
Year of The Crack Mom	$15.00
The Face That Launched a Thousand Bullets	$15.00
The Unusual Suspects	$15.00
Miss Wayne & The Queens of DC	$15.00
Year of The Crack Mom	$15.00
Paid in Blood	$15.00
Shyt List III	$15.00
Shyt List **IV**	$15.00
Raunchy	$15.00
Raunchy 2	$15.00
Raunchy 3	$15.00
Jealous Hearted	$15.00
Quita's Dayscare Center	$15.00
Quita's Dayscare Center 2	$15.00
Shyt List V	$15.00
Deadheads	$15.00
Pretty Kings	$15.00
Pretty Kings II	$15.00
Drunk & Hot Girls	$15.00
Hersband Material	$15.00
Upscale Kittens	$15.00
Wake & Bake Boys	$15.00
Young & Dumb	$15.00
Tranny 911	$15.00
Tranny 911: Dixie's Rise	$15.00
First Comes Love Then Comes Murder	$15.00
Young & Dumb: Vyce's Getback	$15.00
Luxury Tax	$15.00
Mad Maxxx	$15.00
The Lying King	$15.00

Please add $4.00 per book for shipping and handling.
The Cartel Publications * P.O. Box 486 * Owings Mills * MD * 21117

Name: _____

Address: _____

City/State: _____

Contact # & Email: _____

Please allow 5-7 business days for delivery. The Cartel is not responsible for prison orders rejected.

<u>*Personal Checks Are Not Accepted.*</u>